LAND OF HIDDEN FIRES

Praise for Kirk Kjeldsen's Tomorrow City:

"A tight, tense crime novel about a stranger in a strange land trying to outrun the ghosts of his past. Kirk Kjeldsen's Shanghai is a terrifically fresh and evocative setting, and the action jumps off the page."
> - Lou Berney, author of *Whiplash River*, *Gutshot Straight* and *The Long and Faraway Gone*

"Kjeldsen creates drama and danger with ease, and the events that follow are riveting. This is a literary thriller in the best sense of the term… His smart, penetrating story is not to be missed."
> - *The New Jersey Star-Ledger*

"*Tomorrow City* is a vicious little tale of men and violence and the sucking black hole of the past. A coiled and sleek throwback noir, best read in one shot. More please."
> - Elwood Reid, author of *If I Don't Six*, *Midnight Sun*, and *D.B.*

"Kirk Kjeldsen has written a one-sitting novel with an ex-con protagonist you'll eagerly follow across the globe as he tries to shake his past. *Tomorrow City* is as exciting as it is smart as it is heartbreaking."
> - Michael Kardos, author of *The Three Day Affair* and *Before He Finds Her*

"*Tomorrow City* unfolds with grace and power, building to a cinematic climax that reverberates long after you've finished reading. This is thriller writing at its finest. Kjeldsen is one to watch."
> - Carlo Bernard, writer of *The Great Raid* and executive producer / co-creator of *Narcos*

Also by Kirk Kjeldsen

TOMORROW CITY

LAND OF HIDDEN FIRES

A novel
Kirk Kjeldsen

Grenzland Press

Land of Hidden Fires
By Kirk Kjeldsen
Published by Grenzland Press
Copyright © 2017 Kirk Kjeldsen
ISBN: 978-0-9984657-2-2
eBook ISBN: 978-0-9984657-1-5

www.grenzlandpress.com

Cover design: Rafael Andres
Author photograph: SoMi Photographie

for my father,
Richard Christian Kjeldsen (1946-1988);
for Anfinn Michael Oliver Kjeldsen (1903-1984),
a member of the Norwegian resistance
who helped stranded members of the 8th U.S. Air Force
get to Sweden during WWII;
and for Anfinn Michael Oliver Kjeldsen,
my son

*"The surface is calm
in the land of fires,
nothing can be seen,
everything is in balance.*

*But things are in motion
at this moment
like molten avalanches
in the interior mountains.
They know it, those few
who have looked through the fissures
and felt the heat rise."*

-Tarjei Vesaas
(as translated by Anthony Barnett)

CHAPTER 1

The Stjørdalen Valley, Norway
March 1943

Kari looked up from mending a damaged sheep pen when she heard the faint buzzing noise. At first, it sounded like the blackflies that swarmed up from Lake Rømsjøen every summer, but she knew that couldn't be, as it was still weeks before the thaw. She scanned the horizon, looking for the origin of the sound. There was nothing but empty grey space in every direction. Then she looked southward and spotted a fighter plane streaking across the sky. Thick black smoke trailed from its fuselage as it plummeted toward the mountains.

Even if she hadn't seen its Army Air Force markings,

she knew by the whistling sound of its engine that it was a P-47. She'd seen a few in December, over Trondheim, escorting a bomber on its way back to England. She dropped the heavy stone she'd been carrying and hurried back to the barn, clumping through shin-deep snow in men's boots that were two sizes too big for her. Before long, her thin chest ached from sucking in the cold air, but she rushed onward, unable to contain her excitement.

She found her father inside their ramshackle barn, hunched over a thin and sick-looking ewe. Erling Dahlstrøm was a mountain of a man, corded with thick, knotty muscles. Even while kneeling, he was almost the same height as his daughter. Broken-faced and ravaged by life, he looked much older than his forty-one years.

Kari spoke as soon as she entered the barn.

"There's a plane," she said, gasping for breath.

Erling replied in his gravelly voice without looking up.

"Not now."

"But it's the Allies—"

Erling interrupted Kari.

"It's none of our business," he said, finding a swollen and mottled patch of skin on one of the hind legs of the ewe.

"But father—"

Erling snapped at Kari.

"I said no!"

Before Kari could reply, Erling turned his attention

back to the ewe. He unsheathed his knife and lifted the animal's head.

Then he slit its throat.

Kari left the barn, boiling with rage. She got a sledge axe from the shed and went out past the sheep pens to split wood, which she often did when her anger got a hold of her. Though scrawny for a fifteen year-old and scant through the arms and waist, she worked like a man twice her size. Even though the temperature was near freezing, she quickly worked up a sweat, and she peeled off her ratty wool coat to cool down.

She piled one stack of splits and then started in on another, and then another. She kept going until the day turned to night, and the sky had become as purple-black as a bruise. After she finished, she put the axe back in the shed and headed to the barn, where she watered and fed the sheep. It didn't take long, as their dwindling flock was down to seventeen head, or less than a third of what they'd had before Germany had invaded. Most of the sheep that had survived blackleg had succumbed to starvation, and the few that weren't starving had been sold to the Germans in order to keep from losing the farm.

She fed the ewes first, the ones she called Rita and Mae West after her favorite Hollywood stars. In better times, they'd had barley to feed their sheep, but they rarely even had hay anymore and were down to feeding them wheat middlings and by-products they got from a nearby distiller. She fed the rams next, Humphrey and Errol and the Duke, and then their lambs, which she didn't even bother naming, knowing that few would make it to the summer. After she finished with the sheep, she gave some silage to Loki, their old mule, and a bit of hay to Torden, their last horse. Before the war, Erling had had a team of six dun-colored Fjords they'd used for plowing and pulling logs to the river. One by one, they'd sold them off or slaughtered them for food, and they were down to a seventeen-year-old gelding whose best days were behind him.

After finishing with the animals, Kari made her way back to their run-down house. She looked inside one of the hoarfrosted windows and saw her father eating a meager supper at the kitchen table, eyes cast downward and head bowed like a penitent. Wanting to avoid him, she waited outside in the shadows, shivering and blowing on her hands to keep them warm. To pass the time, she traced the old constellations her grandfather had taught her. She spotted Thor's chariot, and the fisherman, and *Ulf's Keptr*, or the mouth of the wolf. She saw the Asar battlefield, the great wagon, and the road of the dead. She could even make out Aurvandil's toe, a sign of spring's coming victory over the winter.

Once she finished counting the stars, Kari looked back through the window and saw Erling leaving the kitchen, taking a lit oil lamp with him. She continued to wait outside until she saw Erling's bedroom door close behind him, then carefully opened the front door and entered the house. She crept into the kitchen and got a husk of stale bread from the pantry, choking it down dry. It wasn't much—before the war, they often had dumplings or herring for lunch, and *gjetost* and brown bread or sliced egg sandwiches nearly every night—and even though she could taste the gritty sawdust they'd mixed in with the wheat to stretch it out, it was far better than rutabaga fried in cod liver oil, or salted horse meat, or even no supper at all, which was often the case since the Germans had invaded.

She washed down the bread with some coppery-tasting pail water. Then she lit another lamp and made her way toward her room, pausing or changing tack every time a board groaned beneath her feet. At one point, she heard her father stirring, and she stopped and waited, afraid that Erling might come out and confront her. But Erling didn't come out, and the stirring soon ceased, and Kari continued on her way.

She got to her room and slipped inside, gently closing the door behind her. Then she put the lamp atop her dresser and took off her sweaters and trousers, stripping to her long underwear. Glancing out the window, she watched the winds file down the snowdrifts, wondering what had happened to the P-47, and whether it had crashed into the mountains. *Surely it couldn't have made it,* she thought to herself. It'd been sinking like a stone, a plume of thick black smoke billowing in its wake. She wondered if the pilot had gone down with the plane, or if the pilot had bailed out, and if the latter, what had happened to him, if he'd actually reached the ground alive.

She finished undressing, then crawled underneath the bed's thick covers and waited for the warmth to come. While she lay there, she glanced over at the Statue of Liberty and Ellis Island postcards that her Uncle Agnar had sent her from New Jersey, where he lived, and the pictures of Clark Gable and Jimmy Stewart that she'd cut out of the *Film Weekly* and *Picturegoer* magazines she'd found at the rubbish heap. She soon found herself thinking about her mother. *What would she have done*, Kari wondered, *if she'd still been alive, and had seen the plane going down?* She'd believed in taking stands, unlike Kari's father. She'd fought for independence from Sweden as a schoolgirl, and she'd demonstrated for suffrage as a young woman. She'd even struggled valiantly against the cancer that had whittled her to a skeleton before claiming her in her thirty-fourth year. She wouldn't have just ignored it.

Kari stared up at the beamed ceiling, unable to sleep. Her thoughts kept circling back to the plane. She turned and looked out the window again, where she saw vacuous shapes merging and breaking apart in the blowing snow.

After a long moment, she got up and pulled on her clothes.

CHAPTER 2

Kari dressed as quietly as she could and draped her covers over her pillow to make it look like she was still sleeping. Then she left her bedroom. She slowly retraced her route back to the kitchen, avoiding the minefield of creaky boards in her path. When she finally got to the front door, she pulled on her ratty overcoat and boots and went outside.

She carefully closed the door behind her, trying not to rouse her father or their flock. Then she made her way across their property, heading in the direction of the mountains. Overhead, the full moon shone like a bowl of fresh cream, luminous and pale. Since she'd gone inside, the temperature had fallen a few more degrees, and she could see her breath crystallizing in the air before her.

She soon passed their crumbling barn. A skittish ewe rustled about inside, then stopped when another ewe bleated at it. After crossing their property, Kari went over the frozen brook that served as a border between their farm and the farm of their neighbors, the Jacobsens, who lived in a large yellow house with electricity and indoor plumbing. There were rumors that the Jacobsens were Quislings, and that they supplied information to the Nazis. They had a herd ten times the size of Erling's, and they even had a number of milking cows, which had been a rarity since the war had broken out.

Kari stayed along the edge of the large property, not wanting to draw the attention of Audr and Odo, the Jacobsen's elkhounds. She breathed a sigh of relief when she finally entered the forest and began to wind her way through the rough country. It was darker there, and quieter; all sounds were buffered by the snow and trees. The heavy boughs of the spruces and pines grew back toward the earth as if gravity had reversed itself, laden with snow and ice. Things moved in the shadows, playing tricks on her eyes; trembling branches became the jangling legs of spiders, and heaving pine boughs became the shaggy beards of trolls.

After a while, a wolf howled in the distance, startling Kari. A chill ran down her spine, and she regretted not putting on another sweater before she'd left their house. She buried her fists in the deep pockets of her woolen coat and continued on her way. Before long, she came across the spaced tracks of a mountain hare, its tiny footfalls barely breaking through the thick crust atop the snow.

Kari soon spotted the splintered crown of a tall spruce in the distance, and then another, and then a knocked-down birch. Her heartbeat quickened, and she picked up her pace. A short distance later, she saw the rudder of the P-47, emerging from a snowdrift like the dorsal fin of a shark. She followed the trail of the wreckage, and she soon came upon a rear gun mount assembly, and then the tail gear axle, and then the wings. Not long after that, she spotted the plane's fuselage. It looked like a bathtub, and it lay crumpled against rocks at the end of a long, deep groove in the frozen earth.

She slowly approached the fuselage. The area around it reeked of gasoline and burnt rubber, stinging her nostrils and eyes. The plane's landing gear was gone, its propeller had sheared off, and the canopy was smashed. The name "MAJOR LANCE MAHURIN" was painted beneath the cockpit window, above six small German crosses, and the words "ROZZIE BETH" were painted in looping red cursive by the nose.

Kari reached forward and touched the side of the plane, expecting to feel heat or vibrations or even electricity. Instead, the riveted steel panel was stone still and as cold as ice. She carefully climbed onto to the tail of the plane and scuttled her way toward the nose. Then she peered into the darkened cockpit, expecting the worst, but she found it empty, other than the shattered pieces of the instrument panel.

She climbed down from the plane and searched the wreck site, looking for footprints or signs of the pilot. There wasn't much, though, other than a headset and a dented canteen. She scanned the area, but there were no further clues. She closed her eyes and turned until she could feel the wind blowing straight at her. Once certain of its path, she set out in the direction it was blowing, assuming that any parachutes would've been carried that way.

Kari pushed deeper into the forest and soon came upon another set of mountain hare tracks. Then she found the mussel-shaped tracks of a roe deer, remembering them from the hunting trips she'd taken with her grandfather. She grew sentimental for a moment, wishing he were there with her, as he'd always seemed to know what to do. But he wasn't there, and there was no chance of him returning from the dead, either, so she shook it from her mind and continued on her way.

Her thoughts soon drifted back toward the pilot. She wondered what he looked like, and where he was from, and if he had someone waiting for him back home. She envisioned him gunning down squadrons of Messerschmitts in spectacular dogfights, handsome and larger than life like Clark Gable in *Night Flight* or Cary Grant in *Only Angels Have Wings*. She'd never seen an American before, other than in magazines or in movies her mother had taken her to see at the Rosendal in Trondheim, and she imagined they must be bigger than Norwegians and Germans somehow, and better looking, as if from some more evolved race or distant planet.

Kari continued to follow the direction of the wind. After walking for almost an hour, the thought occurred to her that she'd brought no weapon. She'd assumed she wouldn't need one—it had been an Allied plane, after all—but then it occurred to her that there might be Germans out looking for the pilot as well. There'd been a strict curfew in effect since 1942, and the penalty for breaking it was severe. She'd heard about the prison camp in Falstad, and the rumors of the torture and executions that had taken place there. One of her neighbors, a schoolteacher, had been sent there in October just for possessing some American newspapers, and no one had heard from the man since.

She grew nauseous, and her knees buckled. She considered turning back, but then realized she'd have just as much chance of running into Germans heading home as she'd have going forward. Continuing on, she made her way through a wooded hill and past an old hunting cabin, then began to make her way down the other side of the hill, soon entering another stretch of forest. Before long, she heard a soft, flapping noise in the distance; it sounded like a flag fluttering in the breeze.

Her heartbeat accelerated, and she felt a cold sweat forming on the back of her neck. The sound grew louder as she continued through the forest, and she soon saw something moving in the distance. At first, she thought her mind was playing tricks on her; it looked like a giant marionette, suspended in mid-air and jerking on its strings. But as she approached it, she realized it was the back of the pilot, hanging from the lines of his parachute, which were tangled up in the branches of a tree.

Kari moved toward the pilot. He heard her crunching footsteps and struggled to turn around, waving a pistol before him. He was no matinee idol, but he was still handsome in an easy, carefree way, with a lanky runner's build and thick, sandy hair slicked back with Brylcream.

"Who's there?" he said, speaking with a slow, country lilt.

Kari stepped forward from the darkness and raised her hands so he could see them.

"Don't shoot," she said.

His eyes narrowed as he sized her up.

"You speak English?" he asked.

She nodded. He lowered the pistol.

"How far am I from Sweden?" he asked.

"Maybe sixty kilometers."

"You know anyone in the resistance?"

She hesitated for a long moment. Then she answered him, surprising even herself with her reply.

"I am," she said.

CHAPTER 3

Snow began to fall. It came down in hard, tiny bits at first that stung the skin and crackled as it hit the trees. Then, as it picked up, it softened, falling like flour from a sifter. Before long, big, saucer-shaped flakes began to flutter down and fill the air, choking out the moonlight.

Kari made her way back to the hunting cabin, a warm, giddy feeling coursing through her. She felt both terrified and exhilarated at the same time, like the time she and her mother went out to the edge of Preikestolen, the towering cliff overlooking the Lysefjord. She pictured herself riding to Sweden with the pilot, and she imagined them falling for each other along the way. She fantasized about him embracing her when they crossed the border, so grateful that he'd offer to take her back to America. She'd decline, of course, out of modesty, but he'd persuade her, promising her a spectacular life in California or wherever it was he was from.

The grumble of a low-flying Heinkel 111 snapped Kari abruptly from her reverie. She looked up just in time to see its distinct, bullet-shaped nose as it rumbled past, presumably on its way to the German base in Trondheim. She picked up her pace and continued on, trudging back up the hill. Before long, she spotted the cabin in the distance.

She approached the cabin just as the moon had begun its descent. The cabin looked like it hadn't been used in years; a snowdrift covered its door, and no smoke rose from its stove chimney. Kari looked in the cabin's only window, but she saw nothing; no light burned inside. She cleared the snow from the door and tried the handle, but it was rusted shut. She tried it again and again, and after a few tries, she finally managed to open it.

Kari stepped inside the cabin. It smelled like old newspaper and mushrooms, and she stumbled over an upturned chair and nearly tumbled to the floor. After righting herself against a table, she continued to grope her way toward the fireplace. She reached for the mantel, grimacing as she felt something fuzzy scuttle away.

She soon found the base of an old oil lamp. After a few matches, she managed to light its nubby wick, filling the room with a soft yellow light. She glanced around at her surroundings; it reminded her of her grandfather's hunting cabin, up on Forbordsfjellet Mountain, where she'd spent her summers as a girl. A narrow bed with a heap of musty blankets occupied one corner of the room, and a few sagging boxes of tools and supplies filled another corner.

Kari approached the boxes of tools and supplies and rummaged through them. She found a rusty sheath knife in one, which she stuffed into her waistband. In the bottom of the other box, she found a coil of rope. She checked the rest of the cabin, looking under the bed and in the small cupboard, but there was nothing else worth taking. Then she left the cabin and hurried her way back to the pilot, following the trail of her vanishing tracks.

At the bottom of the hill, Kari slowed down, not wanting to appear over-eager. She fixed her hair and tried to straighten her coat, ashamed at how shabby it looked. Continuing on, she soon reached the stand of trees where she thought she'd left the pilot, then felt her heart stop when she saw nothing there. Before she could figure out what had happened, a voice called to her nearby, and she turned to see the pilot hanging from another stand of trees.

"Almost thought you forgot me," he said.

Embarrassed, she shook her head.

"You got a name?" he asked.

"Kari," she said.

"I'm Lance Mahurin, of the U.S. Army Air Corps—"

She interrupted him.

"I know," she said.

"How—?"

She interrupted him.

"I saw it on your plane," she said.

"Well now," he said, grinning.

She turned away, trying not to blush. He watched her unwind a few lengths of rope from the coil.

"You sure you don't want to get some help?" he asked.

She nodded, knowing that getting help would mean involving the resistance, which would also mean the end of their time together. She wrapped the end of the rope around her hand, then tossed the coil toward the branches above him. It unraveled after it went over them, and the other end of the rope dropped down within his reach.

"Atta girl," he said.

"Tie it around your waist," she said.

He did. She took the other end of the rope and wrapped it around a nearby tree, then tied the rope around her own waist.

"Now cut the lines," she said. "I'll lower you down."

He pulled a survival knife from a leather scabbard and began to cut his parachute lines. After he severed the last one, the rope went taut, and he dropped down, nearly yanking Kari off her feet.

"Careful," he said.

She dug in and got a firm hold on the rope. Then she slowly walked toward the tree, and as she did, Lance began to lower toward the ground.

Halfway down, Lance noticed the rope was fraying as it rubbed against the bark.

"Watch out—"

Before he could finish, the rope snapped with a rasping crack. Lance fell the last few meters to the ground as Kari tumbled headfirst into the snow. He got up and hurried over to her, helping her to her feet.

"You all right?" he asked.

She nodded as she wiped the snow from her face, her cheeks burning red with embarrassment.

They trudged back in the direction of the farm. Kari occasionally glanced over at Lance, turning away whenever their eyes met. There was so much she wanted to ask him, least of all who Rozzie Beth was, but she didn't know where or how to begin, much less how to phrase it in English. They walked in silence instead, listening to the sound of the wind and the sighing trees.

They wound through the forest until they reached a dry, snow-covered creek. After crossing it, they made their way through a meadow that looked like it'd been slathered with vanilla icing. Before long, they reached the stone wall marking the boundary to the Jacobsen farm. Lance started for the Jacobsen's house, but Kari stopped him and shook her head.

"Quislings," she said.

She moved on, and he followed her. The winds picked up, rustling the naked branches of the trees. Though the sun was still a rumor below the horizon, a weak purple-blue light began to steep into the sky.

They soon came to the frozen brook, and after crossing it, they approached the farm.

"Is this where you live?" asked Lance.

Kari shook her head and looked away.

"It's just some old sheep farmer," she said.

They made their way across the property, past a rotting granary that had been built by Kari's great-grandfather. She stopped when they reached the barn.

"Wait here," she said. "I'll get you some clothes."

Before Lance could reply, Kari left him and approached the house. Then she opened the front door and went in, carefully closing the door behind her. She made her way down the hall, tiptoeing around the creaky boards in her path. When she reached the door to her father's room, she slowly turned the handle and stepped inside.

Kari approached the bed and looked at her father. He seemed so much smaller while sleeping, and so much frailer, bent in upon himself like a folding chair. His jaw was clenched, and his thick arms were wrapped around a pillow, like they were the wings of some wrecked bird protecting its young. She stood there for a moment, feeling pity toward him until she remembered how much she resented him.

Kari went forward and approached the closet. She carefully opened it and looked through her father's clothing; aside from his one, ill-fitting suit, which he hadn't worn since Martha's funeral, his shirts and pants were all variations of the same plain farmer's outfit, and all in muted blacks and greys. She selected the smallest items she could find, which consisted of a pair of patched wool pants, an old pea coat, and a thick cable sweater that Erling seldom wore. Then she closed the closet door and crept her way back across the room.

Before Kari reached the door, Erling stirred, groaning as if he'd been punched in the gut. Kari froze and waited, holding her breath. She watched him wrestle with his sheets, grappling with some invisible foe. After a moment, he settled down again and fell back to sleep, and she continued on her way, leaving the room and quietly closing the door behind her.

She made her way back to the kitchen. Then she opened the cupboard and looked inside. There wasn't much, other than some coarse rye flour, a sack of dried peas, and a few scrawny potatoes. It didn't seem like enough for one person, much less two.

Kari closed the cupboard and took a rusty coffee can down from a shelf. Then she reached into it and pulled a handful of ten and twenty-five øre coins, most of which were zinc, which the government had been using instead of nickel since the Germans had invaded. She counted them, wondering how many she could take without Erling noticing. After a moment, she decided to take them all, then put the empty can back onto the shelf.

She left the house and went back to the barn, where Lance waited, stamping his feet and rubbing his hands.

"Here," she said, handing him the clothes.

"Thanks for your help," he said. "I don't know what I'd have done without you."

She forced a smile and turned away, feeling a growing sense of unease that he was about to leave her. A moment later, he finished changing, and she turned back to face him, startled at how ordinary he appeared without his flight suit. The only things he wore that didn't look like they belonged to a Norwegian farmer were his scuffed jump boots.

"How do I look?" he asked, taking the D-ration bars and cigarettes from his flight suit and stuffing them into the pockets of the pea coat.

"Like a sheep farmer," she said.

He smiled. She smiled back. Another awkward silence passed, and Kari felt the air escaping from her. *Do something*, said a voice in her head, a voice that sounded vaguely like her late mother's. *Do something now, or you'll regret it.*

"So," he said, glancing around at their surroundings. "What's the best way to Sweden?"

"Through the mountains," she said.

"Can you draw me a map?"

She started to nod, out of reflex, then stopped, taking

a moment to compose herself before continuing.

"I can take you," she said, her heart hammering in her chest.

"I can't ask you to do that—"

She interrupted him.

"You don't have to ask," she said, hesitating a moment before adding: "It's my duty."

He smiled, revealing a toothy grin. She forced a smile back, her heart still pounding in her chest. They carried the flight suit behind the barn and put it in an old, stone-lined fire pit. Kari doused it with some kerosene she'd gotten from the barn.

Lance then lit the flight suit with his Zippo, and they silently watched it burn.

CHAPTER 4

The dawn sky filled with a pearly, multicolored light. Thin bands of clouds appeared on the horizon in violet and peach-colored waves. Swifts and other early risers broke the night's silence, rousing from their nests to feed their fledglings. A young ptarmigan took flight from its perch atop a snowdrift, carving a lazy semicircle over the valley before disappearing into the forest.

Kari and Lance rode Erling's rickety cart along an old dirt road. She'd told Lance that the farmer was a friend of the resistance, and that he wouldn't mind them using it. The first lie she'd made had been difficult, twisting her stomach into knots, but each successive fiction had become easier to voice. She'd even started to feel guilty about it, but her guilt was quickly displaced by the exhilaration of being with Lance. He was so much more interesting than the local boys, and he wasn't so timid, like Håkon Grabow, or such a jerk, like Jan Petter Voss.

Torden strained against his reins, huffing little white clouds of hot breath into the cold air. He seemed happy to be out, and to have something to do other than the rote chores they generally gave him. They continued along the dirt road until they reached the Stjørdal River, then followed the river until they picked up a paved country road, which they took east toward Hegra. The roads were empty, and most of them were still buried under the snow. Since the invasion, the only ones allowed to use gas-powered vehicles were police, military, doctors, and administrators, all of which were rarities in the Stjørdalen Valley.

After a while, Lance pulled a battered pack of Lucky Strikes from his pocket. He offered it to Kari.

"Smoke?" he said.

Unwilling to look young or immature, she nodded and took a cigarette from the pack. He pulled out a chrome Zippo with a pair of lightning bolts engraved on the side, beneath the words "*Cave Tonitrum*"—the 56th Fighter Group's emblem—and lit her cigarette before lighting one for himself. She took a short drag, and her lungs tightened. Stifling the urge to cough, she turned away and exhaled, tears forming at the corners of her eyes.

They smoked their cigarettes in silence. Lance flicked away his butt after reducing it to a nub, and Kari did the same, glad to be finished, though she felt a pleasant buzz. They rode onward, and before long, Kari heard a rumbling noise behind them. It sounded like thunderclouds boiling on the horizon. She turned around, and a moment later, she saw two pinpricks of light approaching in the distance. Then she saw two more, and another two after that.

"SS," said Lance, recognizing the vehicles.

They pulled off to the shoulder of the road as a German convoy approached. A pair of four-wheel drive bucket wagons drove out front, their flat-fours straining through the snow. Behind them followed a trio of Opel Blitzes with slatted blackout lights that looked like cats' eyes. A half-track armored personnel carrier pulled up the rear, with gleaming MG-34 machine guns mounted at the front and rear of its open compartment. Kari shuddered, having never seen the Wehrmacht so close.

Her heart pounded in her chest as the convoy drew near. She held her breath, expecting the worst, but the convoy barreled past without slowing. She counted ten grey-uniformed troops in the open compartment of the half-track, and she made fleeting eye contact with one of the sheep-faced troops. She felt sick to her stomach, breathing a sigh of relief when the last vehicle of the convoy disappeared into the distance.

They continued on, approaching the outskirts of Hegra. John Ole Hansen, a farmer from Stjørdal, approached them from the opposite direction, riding a horse-drawn cart full of wooden barrels. He studied them as he drew near, recognizing Kari but not Lance. Kari ignored John Ole as they passed him, looking instead at the road ahead.

They made their way toward the center of town. Kari's eyes widened, startled by the changes that had taken place since she'd been there in December. There were German soldiers everywhere; blood-red flags with large swastikas hung from the flagpoles, having replaced the Norwegian crosses, and posters with regulations in Norwegian and German were plastered up on walls and in shop windows. Dozens of people waited in line for food rations outside the *Handelsforening*, and it looked like the *rådhus* had been taken over. There weren't many locals out, and the few that were seemed to be in a hurry to get where they were going.

They soon approached the train station, a red wooden building the size of a farmhouse. A number of bucket wagons and half-tracks were parked outside, and there were uniformed soldiers everywhere, outnumbering the locals three to one. Kari had never seen so many Germans in one place, other than Trondheim, and Lance noticed her concern.

She pulled the cart to a stop outside a small store.

"Wait here," she said.

Before Lance could reply, Kari climbed down from the cart and went inside. She avoided a pair of Waffen-SS milling about near the front of the store and made her way toward the dry goods in back. Heidrun Ingerø, the proprietor's wife, watched the soldiers from behind the counter, where she restocked the pipe tobacco and cigarettes. It felt tense yet eerily calm to Kari, like the moments typically leading up to a sudden storm.

Kari loitered in the back of the store, trying to overhear the soldiers' conversation. Though she understood some German, as it had replaced English at her school shortly after the Germans had invaded, they spoke with thick accents that sounded Finnish or Russian, and it was hard for her to follow. One of the soldiers said something about an attack on the heavy water plant at Vemork, and the other soldier responded with a phrase Kari didn't understand, though its hostile tone was clear.

Before long, the soldiers approached the cash register and paid for some tinned meat and crackers. Then they left the store. Once they were gone, Kari grabbed a string of sausages, two loaves of bread, and a block of *gjetost* and brought it to the counter. Heidrun frowned.

"I'm sorry, dear, but we don't extend credit—"

Kari interrupted her.

"It's all right," she said. "I have money."

Heidrun watched incredulously as Kari dumped a pile of coins on the counter, along with her battered ration card.

"How much is it?" asked Kari.

"I can give you the sausages or the cheese, but not both," said Heidrun. "And you're only allowed one loaf of bread."

Kari pushed the sausages and one of the loaves of bread forward, and Heidrun tallied the items on a tin register. Kari paid Heidrun without saying a word, then turned and left the store.

She stepped outside, immediately noticing that Lance and the cart were gone. Her knees buckled; she scanned the area, but Lance was nowhere to be seen. She felt bile rise in her throat and stifled the urge to vomit. *Had he been captured?* she wondered. *Or worse—had he just left?* She hurried up a side street, but she didn't see Lance or the cart anywhere. Then she backtracked her way to the train station; the only ones there were Germans, though, other than an older couple and a teenage boy.

She continued on, wondering if he'd been caught, and if so, if she should leave before she was picked up as well. Nearly every fiber of her being was telling her to run, but a small voice told her not to give up, and to keep looking. She rounded a corner and turned onto another side street, and halfway up the next block, she glanced down an alley and saw Lance standing next to the cart. She approached him, out of breath.

"What happened?" she said.

"Some Krauts started nosing around," he replied.

"We better go," she said, climbing up onto the cart. Lance climbed onto the cart after her, and Kari tugged at the reins.

Across the street, Signe Nilsen watched them leave

from the window of her cramped, unheated room in the boarding house. She knew Kari and Erling—she'd even had a crush on Erling in her youth, though it'd been unrequited—and she knew that the man sitting next to Kari wasn't him.

Signe looked toward the *rådhus* across the way, and the Nazi flag that hung outside it, then looked toward her sleeping children, whose breath she could see in the cold air. She hated the idea of helping the Germans, but she hated the idea of losing another child to illness even more.

She pulled on her threadbare jacket and made her way to the door, then quietly opened it and left the room.

CHAPTER 5

He saw her from the top of a ridge, where he'd been stalking an eight-point buck. Or at least he saw what he thought was her, sitting at the edge of Lake Rømsjøen with her back to him, staring into its black depths. She looked as beautiful as she had the moment he'd first laid eyes on her, at the *Sankthansaften* festivities back in the summer of 1917. Her long, unfastened hair was the color of autumn wheat, an ungovernable tangle of curls that were the envy of all of her friends, and the desire of all of his.

He could have stared at her forever, even just the back of her, and he probably would have, too, had she not suddenly rose and pitched forward into the water, collapsing like an animal that'd been heartshot. After she disappeared beneath the lake's gently rolling surface, he dropped his *tennstempel* rifle and bolted in her direction, running downhill through the dense forest. Contrary to what he'd expected, though, the further he ran, the more difficult it became, until it felt like he was trudging uphill through knee-deep mud.

The forest grew thicker and darker all around him. He opened his mouth to scream, but no sounds came. It was as if he'd forgotten how to speak, as if his vocal cords had been severed. He tried again and again in vain, and the forest rose up and folded over him, burying him like a tidal wave.

Erling woke with a start, gasping for air. He glanced around the bedroom and got his bearings, realizing he'd only been dreaming. He shook the thoughts of Martha from his mind, then sat up and swung his knotty legs over the side of the bed. His arthritic knee throbbed like a beating heart, and he kneaded it until the pain finally subsided.

He dressed in the near-darkness, pulling on the same clothes he'd worn the previous day. His bones ached to the marrow, and he felt like he was seventy-five years old. After he laced up his boots, he picked up his scuffed pocket watch and glanced at its face. It was almost six o'clock, a full hour later than he normally slept. He shook his head and left the room, knowing that the animals would be agitated.

He went out into the hallway and approached Kari's door. Then he knocked and waited, but there was no reply. He'd stopped opening her door unannounced years before—he was certain she'd had her first monthly visit, though he'd had no idea how to discuss the subject with her nor any desire to, either. Whatever it was, he gave her some space, which seemed to be the only way he knew how to deal with her anymore.

Erling continued on into the kitchen. He put some wood into the stove and lit it, and put on a kettle. While waiting for the water to boil, he glanced out a window and watched the sun rise. Few things in life gave him as much pleasure, other than reading Jack London novels and smoking his pipe on the rare occasions he had tobacco.

After the water reached a boil, Erling poured it over the roasted chicory he'd been using as a coffee substitute since the rationing had begun. Then he poured himself a cup of the bitter brew and cut it with some sheep's milk. He choked it down as fast as he could, chasing the acrid taste with a dipper of pail water. Then he pulled on his coat and went outside to begin the chores.

He made his way across the property and approached the barn. One of the rangy forest cats that haunted their farm darted across his path, presumably in pursuit of a wood mouse. Erling watched it disappear into the underbrush, then approached the barn door and slid it open.

The first thing he noticed, after seeing that another sheep showed signs of blackleg, was Torden's empty stall.

Erling headed back behind the barn. Before he got there, he already knew the cart was gone, seeing the fresh tracks in the snow. At first, he couldn't imagine where Kari could have gone, or why she would've gone anywhere at all. Then he remembered her excitement over the downed Allied plane. He turned and made his way back toward the house, inwardly cursing himself for having been so dismissive.

He went inside and got his thick hat and an extra sweater from his closet, noticing then that some of his clothes were missing. After putting on the hat and sweater as well as his thickest coat, he went back out to the barn and fed the sheep. Then he got a worn saddle down from a peg on the wall and approached Loki's stall. The head-shy mule backed away from him, stamping nervously at the frozen earth.

Erling put down the saddle and slowly approached Loki, stroking the mule's face and quietly talking to him. He told him that everything was fine, and that he'd never let anyone hurt him. It was so much easier for him to talk to animals than to people, and it always had been, since he'd been a boy. After a moment, Loki's ears softened, and his breathing returned to normal. He even began to nuzzle Erling's hand, hungry for his touch.

Once Loki was calm, Erling gently placed the saddle upon Loki's back. Then he buckled the saddle and led Loki away from the barn, heading off in the direction of the cart tracks. He hesitated when he reached the dirt road, and he stood there for a long moment, internally debating with himself over whether or not he should bring his rifle. If the Germans were to find him with it, they would execute him on the spot, as the penalty for possessing firearms was death. But if Kari was in any sort of trouble and he had no way of helping her, he'd never be able to forgive himself for having no weapon.

After a long moment, Erling tied Loki to a tree, then turned and made his way back to the house. He went inside and went into his bedroom, then squatted down, lifted up the corner of the threadbare rug, and pried up a loose floorboard. He reached into the hidden space beneath the floorboard, but there was nothing there; he ran his hand over the space again and again, but he still found nothing, other than cobwebs. His stomach dropped. *What if the Nazis had found it?* he wondered. There's no way they would've just let him live. *Or would they? Were they watching him, and waiting, planning on using him for something else?*

He continued to grope blindly in the darkness, and after a long moment, his fingertips found the rifle. He grabbed it by its stock and slowly pulled it out, breathing a sigh of relief when he saw its barrel glinting in the light. He reached back into the crawl space and soon found a half-empty box of rifle cartridges. He shook the cartridges from the box and slipped them into his pocket, then put the floorboard back in place and covered it with the rug.

Erling rolled up the rifle in a bedroll and slung it over

his shoulder, then made his way into the kitchen and took the rusty coffee can down from the shelf. He found it empty, though, aside from a one-krone coin. He took the coin and put the can back on the shelf, then filled his pockets with the last of their crackers and jerky. Then he left the house and made his way back to the dirt road.

Erling approached Loki and untied him from the tree. Then he led him to the dirt road and mounted up, and Loki lurched off, struggling under Erling's weight. Erling hadn't ridden the mule in years, and with each jostling step, his knee felt like someone was shoving an ice pick through it, but he nudged the mule onward, trying to make up time. Before long, Loki worked up a pasty sweat, and he started to act skittish again after sliding on a patch of ice. Erling gently patted Loki's neck and whispered into his ear, and the mule settled down.

Erling guided Loki onward toward the frozen brook. He cut a wide berth around the border to the Jacobsen's farm, not wanting them to see him and wonder why he was out riding a mule on a weekday morning. He then came toward the edge of Hjalmar Prestrud's small farm, and for a moment, he considered asking to borrow a horse and cart from his old friend. Then he rejected the idea, afraid it might only raise questions, since he hadn't called on Hjalmar in years.

He nudged Loki onward, up a hill and then down into a tree-choked valley. He soon emerged from the forest and reached the paved country road. He looked westward, toward Trondheim, then looked east, to Hegra and Sweden beyond it. It seemed unlikely that Kari would be heading toward Trondheim, which had a large German airfield and a submarine base as well.

After a moment, Erling set off east in the direction of Hegra.

A wall of clouds rolled in overhead, blotting out the sun. The valley appeared as if it was twilight, even though it wasn't yet noon. Most of the birds had already retreated to their nests, fooled into thinking the day was prematurely ending. A few hardy ones remained, though, their lonesome songs piercing the silence.

Erling arrived at the outskirts of town just as the storm clouds began to gather, bunching like bed sheets after a long and sleepless night. He left the main road and made his way back behind an abandoned barn, where he tied his bedroll to Loki's saddle and then tied Loki to a fencepost, not wanting anyone to know he hadn't ridden in on his cart. Loki started to stamp his feet again and tug at the rope, but Erling whispered some Jonas Lie poems into Loki's ear and patted his neck. After a while, Loki settled again, and Erling left him some chaff to pick at before heading into town.

The winds came howling down from the mountains, chilling Erling to the bone. He pulled his hat down low and buried his fists into his pockets. One of the townspeople said hello and smiled at him as he approached. Erling forced a smile back at the man as he continued past.

He soon turned onto the main street. There were more Germans in Hegra than the last time he'd been there, multiplying like the stubborn sow thistle that plagued their barley fields. Before the war, nothing had ever happened in the small village, other than a local priest getting elected bishop of Bergen and the opening and subsequent closing of the nearby Hegra Fortress, a defense built to thwart a Swedish attack that had never materialized. Now, it was a regular stop for the Nazis, halfway between their bases in Trondheim and the Swedish border. Every time Erling returned to the village, more and more soldiers seemed to be arriving from Sweden by train, despite Sweden's so-called neutrality in the war.

Erling walked through the small town, glancing down each alley and side street for his cart. He checked the train station, assuming that Kari and the pilot might've tried to take a train to Sweden, an occasional but risky strategy of the resistance. It wasn't there, though; the only vehicles outside the station belonged to the Germans. He checked the Buland house after that, where Kari's schoolmate Marit lived with her mother and father, but it wasn't there, either. He even tried the church, which he'd been avoiding since Martha's funeral. He approached it from the rear, so he wouldn't have to see her small headstone in the graveyard out front, but the mere sight of the whitewashed chapel took his breath away. Fortunately for him, though, there were no cart tracks leading to or away from the church, and there were no carts parked outside it, either. He turned around before even getting within a hundred yards of the church, his disappointment over not finding Kari there overshadowed by his relief of not having to visit Martha's grave.

He made his way back to the center of town and spotted the grocery store. Perhaps Kari had stopped there, he thought to himself. He went inside the store and looked over the dry goods while an SS officer lectured Per Ingerø, the spindly proprietor, about the price of whiskey. Not wanting to anger the officer, Per gave him the whiskey for free. The officer then left the store, shaking his head and muttering curses under his breath.

As soon as the officer was gone, Erling grabbed a container of oats and made his way to the counter. Embarrassed by the encounter with the German, Per averted his eyes from Erling's, though he still had the courtesy to address him.

"Good day," he said.

"Good day," said Erling, placing the oats on the counter.

"Will that be all?" asked Per.

Erling wanted to ask if Per had seen Kari, but he didn't want to raise any suspicion, so he just nodded.

"Thirty øre," said Per.

Erling pulled out the only coin he had and gave it to Per. Per gave him his change, and after a long moment, Erling just blurted it out, unable to think of any other way to say it.

"Did Kari come by today?" he asked.

Per shook his head.

"I haven't seen her," he said.

Before Erling could reply, Heidrun spoke from the back of the store.

"She came by, all right," she said.

Erling turned to look as Heidrun emerged from the back of the store.

"She bought bread and cheese, and she wanted to buy sausages, too," said Heidrun.

"I asked her to get something for my cousin," said Erling, saying the first thing that came to mind. "He's coming from Eidum, to help with the lambing."

"A bit early for that, isn't it?" said Heidrun, questioning him with a glance.

"We mated early," said Erling, returning her glance with a hard stare. Heidrun's eyes narrowed again, but Erling took his things and left the store before it could go any further.

He made his way back across town, burning inside. Even though it was a small village, it felt like it took him hours to cross. He figured Kari must have been trying to make it to Sweden with the pilot. *How much of a head start did she have?* he wondered. *An hour? Two, or three, or even four?* He fought the urge to run, knowing it would only draw more attention.

Erling soon left the village. He went back behind the barn, untied his bedroll from the saddle, and slung it over his shoulder. Then he untied Loki from the fencepost and led him toward the road.

Once he reached the road, Erling mounted the mule and tugged sharply at the reins, and Loki trotted off. While Erling rode away, Sverre Hattestad approached the barn on a rusty old bicycle with thick rope in place of its tires, fighting his way through the snow. Scraggly and unkempt with *snus*-stained teeth and a patchy beard, he was little more than a sack of muscle wire and bone, chiseled lean from a lifetime chasing things he'd already lost and things he wouldn't ever have. He pulled his bicycle over to the side of the road and watched Erling ride off on his mule, and he narrowed his gaze, suspicious.

Then he turned and looked back in the direction of the *rådhus*.

CHAPTER 6

A cow moose and its reedy calf wandered through the hills above Trondheim, chewing the bark and low branches off the trees at the outskirts of the city. Spotting some early fireweed emerging from a snowdrift, the calf stumbled toward the forest's edge and gorged itself, oblivious to the houses nearby. Its mother trotted forward and nudged the calf back toward the tree line, and just as quickly as they'd appeared, they disappeared back into the forest.

Down in the center of Trondheim, Wehrmacht Oberleutnant Conrad Moltke stood at the window of his luxurious room in the Stiftsgården, frowning as he watched the activity on Dronningens Gate. It wasn't the accommodations that made him unhappy, as the palatial rooms were by far the most luxurious lodging he'd ever had. It wasn't the weather, either, which was no worse than the perpetual rain that drenched his home city of Berlin. It also wasn't the duties that awaited him that morning, which could've been performed with ease by any of his junior, non-commissioned staff. What caused his disappointment was that he believed he should've been elsewhere by then, perhaps fighting with Rommel in North Africa, or with Manstein on the Eastern Front. The son of an Lieutenant Colonel who'd received the Iron Cross for his service at Gallipoli, and the grandson of a Field Marshall who'd received the Crown Order and the *Pour le Mérite* for his gallantry during the Austro-Prussian War, his only goal in life had been to follow in their footsteps and distinguish himself on the battlefield. His one mistake, however, had been hesitation—he'd wavered before joining the NSDAP, when far less-talented men like Josef Terboven, his superior and the Reichskommissar for Norway, had leapt at the chance. Even after joining in 1931, which was still two years before the NSDAP had come into power, his earlier hesitation would never be forgiven, so instead of getting the chance to prove himself in battle, Moltke had been relegated to babysitting duties at the far edge of the Reich.

He took a sip of the coffee that had been brought to him and winced. It tasted lousy, more like hot dish water than what he'd been accustomed to in Germany. He put it aside and approached his collection of gramophones, which he'd brought from Berlin. *Thank God for my music,* he thought to himself. After browsing through them, he selected a recording of Mozart's Piano Concerto No 22 in E-Flat major, performed by Edwin Fischer. Though the Nazis, who found it too cosmopolitan for their tastes, didn't approve Mozart, Moltke vastly preferred him to Wagner, Bruckner, and the rest of Hitler's favorites, whom he found bombastic and trite.

He slid the gramophone from its dust sleeve and carefully placed it onto the Victrola's turntable. Then he lowered the needle and waited for it to play. Before long, the opening notes of the andante movement tumbled forth from the Victrola's speaker horn. Moltke closed his eyes and thought back to Berlin in the early twenties, after he'd graduated from the *Preußische Kriegsakademie,* when Elise was still with him. He'd felt like he had it all when he'd been out with her, walking the tree-lined Kurfürstendamm or having drinks at the Romanisches Café. *If only things had gone differently*, he thought to himself. *If I'd only been more resolute, or if I'd been able to foresee what was coming.*

After a moment, someone knocked on the door, shattering his fantasy. The colorful avenues of Charlottenburg fell away in his mind to reveal the dour, grey streets of Trondheim, and Elise vanished like smoke in the wind. A voice spoke out in the hallway, and Moltke opened his eyes, grimacing when he saw the amateurish oil panting of Queen Sophie above his bed.

"Herr Oberleutnant?"

He said nothing, hoping the man would just go away if he ignored him, but the man remained.

"I have a message for you," said the man, knocking again.

Moltke continued to ignore him.

"Herr Oberleutnant?"

Moltke finally trudged over to the Victrola and lifted the needle from the gramophone, bringing the soothing music to a halt.

"Come in," he said in a resigned voice.

The door opened, and Otto Blücher, an oafish corporal, burst into the room. He stumbled on the edge of a thick rug, bumping into a table and spilling Moltke's coffee onto a sheaf of papers.

"*Verdammte Scheiße!*" said Moltke, grabbing the papers before the coffee ruined them.

"Sorry, sir—"

Moltke interrupted him.

"What do you want?" he said, using a handkerchief to wipe up the coffee.

"We just got word from command," said Blücher. "They found a downed Allied plane nearby, in the mountains."

"So go look at it."

"The Major wants you to go," said Blücher. "He said it's urgent."

Moltke groaned and closed his eyes again.

"Herr Oberleutnant?" said Blücher.

Ignoring him, Moltke tried to envision springtime in Charlottenburg once more, and Elise on his arm. But all he could see were thousands of smirking, goose-stepping Hitlers, marching up the Kurfürstendamm and saluting him as they went past.

They took a pair of half-tracks out to the crash site. There weren't any paved roads after Hommelvik, and the Opel Blitzes they normally drove didn't get far in the snow and mud. The half-tracks were slow, though, and they were barely capable of doing thirty kilometers per hour, even over flat ground. By the time they finally entered the Stjørdal forest, the sun was directly above them, though hidden behind a wall of clouds.

Blücher rode out front with three other enlisted men. Moltke rode behind in the second vehicle, preferring to bring up the rear in case they came across any land mines planted by the resistance. He was accompanied by his driver, Ulrich Schweitzer, a narcissistic Olympic swimmer more interested in deflowering locals than the actual war, and Manfred Goetz, a whey-faced, alcoholic worm Moltke suspected of being a pedophile. Between the cloying sweetness of Schweitzer's cheap 4711 cologne and the overpowering stench of Goetz's body odor, Moltke found himself fighting the urge to throw up since they'd left Trondheim. He sat as far back in the half-track as he could, chain-smoking and staring out at the landscape as it scrolled past.

They stopped about a kilometer from the crash site when it became impossible to proceed with the half-tracks. Then they set out on foot, hiking their way through the uneven country. Blücher took the point, bounding forward through the snow like a St. Bernard off its leash. Goetz and the other enlisted men followed, fingers resting above the triggers of their machine guns in case they came across the resistance or the Inter-Allied Commandos.

Moltke smoked another cigarette as he followed the column. He glanced around at their surroundings and couldn't help but frown again. It was certainly beautiful, he had to admit; it even reminded him of the Arlberg, where he and his older brothers had spent their childhood winters skiing at Zürs and St. Christoph. But beauty wasn't the point of war, and he wasn't on a vacation, either. He needed to come up with a way to get to Kharkov, where they were fighting the Red Army, or the North African desert, to do battle on the roads Julius Caesar and Alexander the Great had once travelled—and he needed to do it soon, before it was too late.

After a while, Blücher broke into a trot when he saw the split tops of some trees in the distance. The others picked up their paces as well, and they soon came upon the rudder of the P-47. They followed the trail of wreckage until they reached the crash site, where a fresh-faced soldier wearing a trench coat two sizes too big for him sat shivering next to the plane's fuselage. The boy jumped to his feet when he saw Moltke approaching and gave him an enthusiastic Nazi salute.

"Heil Hitler!" said the boy.

"Yeah, yeah," said Moltke, responding with a half-hearted wave and glancing around. "So, where is he?"

"Who?"

"The pilot, you ass. Who do you think?"

"He must've bailed out, sir."

"You don't say?"

The boy shook his head, failing to register Moltke's sarcasm. Schweitzer scanned their surroundings.

"He couldn't have gotten far," he said.

Moltke turned to his men.

"Search the area," he said.

Blücher and one of the enlisted men headed west into the forest, while Goetz and another enlisted man went east toward a valley. Schweitzer went north toward the mountains with the last enlisted man, and Moltke lit another cigarette and followed them from a distance.

They walked through the untouched snow. After a while, Moltke's stomach began to whine. He generally skipped the Norwegian breakfasts, which consisted of gamy goat cheese and dried fish, preferring to wait for his cook to make him a German meal, perhaps a *schnitzel* if they had any veal, or maybe some *sauerbraten* if they didn't. Hopefully they'd find the downed pilot before long, and preferably dead, as that meant less paperwork, so Moltke could get back to his music. Maybe he'd even have a cigar and open the bottle of Hennessy he'd been saving, the one he'd confiscated from the textile importer in Bergen.

They soon came to a wooded hill, and after reaching its crest, they spotted the old hunting cabin. Seeing some recent footprints around the cleared-away cabin door, Schweitzer crept forward and looked through a frost-covered window. Then he gave a signal to the enlisted man, who kicked open the door and stormed inside with his machine gun raised.

Moltke waited outside and finished his cigarette as Schweitzer followed the enlisted man inside. He decided he'd write another letter to the Brigade General when he got back to Trondheim, requesting a transfer to the front. It didn't matter which one—any front would do. Then he changed his mind and decided to go straight to the General. It wasn't an orthodox move, but it was time to take a risk, whatever the costs might be. *Hoffen und harren macht manchen zum Narren*, he thought to himself, which had been a favorite saying of his grandfather. *He that lives on hope shall die fasting.*

After a moment, Schweitzer and the enlisted man emerged from the cabin, shaking their heads. Then they lowered their machine guns and set off into the forest. Moltke dropped his cigarette butt to the snow and followed them. They trudged through the woods, down the other side of the hill and into another stretch of thick pines and birch trees.

They continued to scour the forest, but there were no tracks anywhere, and no signs that anyone had recently been there, either. After emerging from the forest and crossing a meadow, they reentered the wilderness and began to circle back toward the others. Before long, Moltke saw the cut parachute lines in the branches above them.

"Sir," said Schweitzer.

Moltke turned and looked in the direction Schweitzer was pointing and saw two faint sets of tracks leading away from the area. One set was similar in size to their own tracks.

The other set of tracks were smaller, though, as if they'd belonged to a child.

CHAPTER 7

The Stjørdal River snaked its way westward through the hills and lowlands of the valley. A narrow dirt road trailed alongside it, following the river like a shadow. At times, the snow covering the road became crisscrossed with tire tracks, signs of the fleeing resistance or the Germans in pursuit. In other places, it was unmarked by wheel or hoof or even boot, and it became difficult to tell where the road ended and where the wilderness began.

Kari and Lance rode the rest of the morning without stopping, and they kept riding into the afternoon. She made them sandwiches as the sun began to drop toward the western hills, cutting the bread and cheese as thin as shingles so it would last. They didn't stop to eat or rest, washing it down with handfuls of snow they scooped up along the way. Unused to the workload, Torden faltered at times, but Kari spurred him onward, tugging at the reins.

After making their way up a low rise, they pushed down into a valley. A blackened farmhouse stood at the edge of a field, an act of reprisal by the Germans and a warning against defiance. Most of the farmhouse's roof was caved in and one of its walls had collapsed, and Kari could see into what looked like a child's room, judging by some blackened wallpaper and a scorched crib. She wondered what had happened to the child who'd slept there and shuddered. Then she shook the thought from her mind as they continued on their way.

The road diverged from the river as it descended into the craggy bowl of the countryside. After the terrain evened out, the road twisted back toward the water as if somehow drawn to it, and the road and the river met up again in another broad valley. Soon, in the distance, Kari and Lance spotted a one-lane bridge spanning the water. Well before reaching it, they could see that half of it was missing; a few of the limestone piers that had supported it had been reduced to rubble, and some of its ironwork lay in pieces in the ice below.

Kari pulled up on Torden's reins, and they came to a stop.

"Is there another place to cross?" asked Lance.

"There's a bridge downriver at Mælen, but that's at least a day out of the way."

"What about upriver?"

Kari shook her head and looked toward the ice.

"Maybe we should try to cross here," she said.

Before Lance could reply, Kari got down from the cart and approached the river. She tapped the ice with her foot a few times, and it felt solid enough, so she walked out a few paces. The ice held, so she tapped it again with her foot, harder and harder until she was practically stomping on it, but it remained firm.

"It feels all right to me," said Kari.

Lance climbed down from the cart and walked onto the ice, testing it for himself. Kari walked past him and approached Torden, who shifted nervously from side to side. She patted his nose and whispered into his ear, a skill she'd learned from her father, and before long, Torden ceased rocking. Kari then took the reins and led Torden to the riverbank, where Lance waited.

"One of us should go first and make sure it's okay," he said.

"You go," she said, taking the coil of rope from the back of the cart and putting it over her shoulder. "I'll follow with the horse."

"You sure?"

She nodded. He took the rest of their items from the back of the cart to lighten its load, then slowly walked out onto the ice.

Lance walked a dozen paces, testing the ice after he got about ten meters out. The ice held. He looked back at Kari and smiled, and she followed him onto the ice, leading Torden with as much rope as the reins afforded. Torden stopped when he reached the river's edge and hesitated, unsure, and Kari turned back to face him.

"It's okay," she said.

Torden snorted and shook his head, remaining where he was. Kari walked back toward him and patted him on the nose, whispering again into his ear. Then she turned around and walked out onto the ice, tugging gently at the reins.

Torden took a small step forward, following Kari, and when he realized the ice would hold, he took another small step, and then another. Just ahead of them, Lance continued to make his way toward the center of the river. He progressed carefully and deliberately, scanning the ice for thin patches or cracks. After a while, he turned around and looked back at Kari, grinning, and she forced an uneasy smile back. Then he turned around and looked forward again, toward the other side of the river. It seemed like it was a long way away, even though it couldn't have been more than fifty meters.

A third of the way across the frozen river, Torden's front right foot slipped as he stepped down onto the ice. Kari's heart skipped a beat as Torden stopped short, snorting again and raising his ears. She closed her eyes and took a deep breath, knowing that Torden could sense her fear, and that he'd panic if he thought she was afraid. She held the breath as long as she could and then slowly let it out, and after the feeling passed, she opened her eyes again and nudged him onward.

Lance soon passed the center of the river, walking around a buckled iron railing that rose from the broken ice dam like a makeshift cross. He spotted an uneven patch of ice before him where some floes crashed and piled together before freezing over. After changing his direction, he turned back and pointed them out to Kari. She changed her direction as well, advancing step by agonizing step.

Kari approached the center of the river. Realizing she'd reached the point furthest from either shore, she felt both elation and dread, and the combination made her nauseous. She suppressed the urge to throw up and continued on, and just after crossing the center of the river, the ice strained and cracked beneath her. Torden stopped short at the sound, and he snorted again and shook his head.

Lance turned around and saw Kari, registering the terror in her eyes.

"Stay calm," he said.

"Where's the crack?" she said, glancing around and struggling to keep from hyperventilating.

"I don't know."

They looked for fissures in the ice, but they didn't find any. Torden shifted back and forth and started to slip, and Kari struggled to calm him down.

"Keep moving," said Lance.

She tugged at Torden's reins and resumed walking, and Torden skittishly followed her, slipping and sliding on the ice. The more he lost his footing, the more panicked he became; Kari quickly went from struggling to keep him calm to merely holding onto the reins.

Lance picked up his pace and approached the opposite side of the river. Before he could reach it, he heard a loud crack somewhere to his right. Then he heard another crack somewhere to his left, and he watched in disbelief as a jagged split ran past him like a lightning bolt, fracturing the ice.

He turned back to Kari.

"Stay where you are," he said.

She froze, and they waited, holding their breath. Seconds passed as slowly as hours, and for a brief moment, Kari thought the ice might actually hold. But then they heard another crack, and then another, even louder one, like a gunshot. Torden whinnied and rose up on his back feet, and as the ice collapsed beneath him, he sank past his hips and began struggling for purchase.

"Run!" shouted Kari.

Lance turned and bolted for the riverbank. Kari made a break for it as well, sidestepping a hole that opened in the fracturing ice, and then another, and another. Torden shrieked and whinnied as he thrashed about, trying to get his footing so he could continue on, but the more the ice broke beneath him, the more water flooded up, and they were all soon slipping and sliding in the shifting mess.

Lance reached the riverbank first and scrambled onto solid ground. He turned and looked back to see Kari approaching, struggling through the ice and water. Ten meters from reaching the edge of the river, her right foot plunged through the ice and she sank to her thigh. She struggled to pull her leg free, and after she finally managed to do so, she got back to her feet and continued on.

Just as Kari reached the bank of the river, Torden shrieked behind her, fifteen meters from shore. It was a horrible sound, like that of a person being eviscerated while alive. Kari looked back and saw that both of Torden's back legs and the cart had broken through, and he was struggling to pull himself up onto a tilting shelf of ice, only to sink deeper and deeper into the frigid water. She took the rope off her shoulder and tied one end of it around her waist, then handed the rest of the coil to Lance.

"Tie this to a tree," she said.

"Wait," he said, reaching for her arm, but she was already back on the ice, stumbling toward the horse. After a few steps, Kari slipped off an ice shelf and plunged into the water. It was colder than anything she'd ever felt, and all the air left her lungs in an instant, as if a giant fist had squeezed her. She dog-paddled the rest of the way to Torden, who thrashed about in a panic, struggling to pull himself back onto the ice only to break it up even more. Once she finally reached him, he nearly kicked her in the face with a blow that would've killed her had it landed. She swam her way around him through the ice-choked water, giving him as wide a berth as possible so he couldn't kick her or get tangled in the rope.

Kari patted Torden on the side of the neck when she reached him and whispered into his ear.

"Easy, boy," she said to him. "I'm not going to hurt you."

He snorted and shook his head, but she kept patting him and started to sing a lullaby her mother had sung to her when she was a girl.

Mamma tar meg på sitt fang,
danser med meg att og fram.
Danse så, med de små,
danse så, så skal barnet sove...

Torden continued to thrash about in the frigid mess, so she sang the lullaby again, whispering it into his ear. By the time she finished, Torden was finally beginning to calm down. She took out the sheath knife she'd found in the cabin, holding it behind her back so Torden wouldn't see it. Then she began to cut the lines of the harness that bound him to the cart.

Over on the riverbank, Lance wrapped the rope around a tree trunk and tied it fast. After she finished cutting the lines of the harness, Kari grabbed Torden by the mane and pulled herself up onto his back. He tried to buck her off, but she held on, and she signaled to Lance to start pulling them.

Lance dug his heels into the ground and tugged at the rope. Torden struggled to climb out of the water and onto the ice, but he only ended up breaking off another shelf and plunging back into the freezing river. He thrashed and brayed again, and Kari struggled to hold on.

"Keep pulling," she said.

Lance wrapped the rope around his fists and pulled again, and Torden fought his way up and onto the ice. Again, it broke from his weight, but he managed to climb forward onto the next bit of ice, which also broke, and then the next bit, where the water was shallow enough for him to stand. Finally gaining some traction, Torden struggled forward on his own, fighting through the icy shallows and onto solid ground. Kari jumped down from Torden's back and watched him clamber up the riverbank and out into a snow-covered field, kicking and thrashing like a bucking bronco.

Then she looked back at the river, and she watched her father's cart disappear below the ice-choked surface of the water.

CHAPTER 8

Dark, heavy clouds loomed over the eastern mountains, swollen like sausages and ready to burst. A keening wind howled down from the hills, filing the snowdrifts smooth and erasing the bird tracks and deer sign. It was cold, stone-cracking cold, the kind of cold that hurt deep inside the lungs. The world seemed flattened, buried under a landslide of grey.

Sverre Hattestad rode his rusty bicycle off the paved country highway and onto an old dirt road. He struggled to grip the bicycle's handlebars, his bare fingers numb from the cold. Strings of gluey *snus* dribble froze in his beard, and his yellow teeth rattled like wind chimes in a storm.

He turned off the dirt road and onto a narrow cart

path. Though it'd been years since he'd been in the area, he still knew its roads and paths as if he'd never left. As a boy, he'd been a friend of Erling, Christian Jacobsen, and Hjalmar Prestrud; his family's dairy farm was in between theirs, near a tributary of the Leksa. They'd gone to Sunday school together at the Hegra Church, and they'd spent their winters skiing and hunting grouse in the Skarvan Mountains. They'd been inseparable until a few bad summers had forced Sverre's father to sell their farm, which had been in the Hattestad family for six generations. After the family had moved to a small apartment in town, Sverre's father left to work on the whaling ships up in Svalbard, and he never came back, leaving fourteen year-old Sverre to take care of his mother and three sisters. Sverre dropped out of school and went to apprentice for a local baker, and the boys lost touch, eventually becoming strangers who didn't even bother greeting in town.

The cart path dipped around a bend, then rose up a slight incline through the hillocked forest. Sverre pedaled as hard as he could, but the snow was deep and thick, forcing him to hop off the bicycle when it came to a standstill. He push-started the bicycle and managed to pedal it a few more times before it came to another stop. Then he climbed down from the bicycle, racking with a fit of coughing, and pushed it onward, continuing on foot.

He left the cart path after passing the dirt road leading to the Prestrud farm and made his way through the darkening forest. Walking the bicycle through the woods took twice as long as walking it along the path, and it took twice as much energy, but the thought of seeing his family's farm made his stomach turn. Once he was certain he was well past the property, and past the old apple orchard next to it where he used to read *Captain Marryat* novels and had his first kiss with Solveig Nielsen, he emerged from the forest and resumed pushing his bicycle along the path. Before long, he spotted the Dahlstrøm farmhouse in the distance. Even though it'd been decades since he'd seen it, it was exactly as he'd remembered.

Sverre leaned the bicycle against a tree and looked toward the farm. A flood of memories washed over him. Here were the birch trees they'd cut branches from to whittle arrows, and there was the granary where they'd hide their slingshots and bawdy French postcards; over there was the hayloft where they'd slept during the endless July nights, and at the edge of the forest was the old foot path that wound down to the lake, where they'd swim and fish for grayling and wild trout. Of all the boys in the valley, Erling had been Sverre's closest friend; Sverre had followed Erling around like a dog, even though they were the same age. Whereas he was slight and weak, Erling was strong and rugged; while he was nervous and insecure, Erling was confident and liked by all. Sverre had looked up to Erling as if he was his older brother, which had made Erling's abandonment of him even more painful than the rest.

He made his way to the rear of the farmhouse, staying close to the tree line and its long shadows. If they were indeed harboring the downed pilot, he first needed proof. The last thing he wanted to do was to lose favor with the Germans; despite disagreeing with their politics, he saw them as his only hope of getting another chance, since no one in Hegra would even look at him. He could live with himself ignoring some of the Nazi's excessive ways and means; living hand to mouth any longer seemed like a far more unpalatable fate.

Sverre left the tree line when he reached the back of the farmhouse and crept his way toward the cellar door. He looked up at the rusty chimney on the farmhouse's slanting roof; no smoke rose from it, but that didn't mean there wasn't anyone inside. If anything, if they were hiding someone, he figured they'd go out of their way to seem like they weren't.

He made his way toward a window, advancing at an angle in case anyone was standing near it. Then he slowly peered in, but there was nothing to see—the kitchen and living room were both empty. He walked around the house, looking inside each window more openly than the last. He didn't see anyone, though, nor any lamps or fires, despite being past the hour most families retired.

Before long, Sverre reached the point he'd started from, noticing that his own halting footprints were the only ones marring the snow. If the snow had started falling midday, he presumed, then it appeared that no one had been there since morning. He left the house and walked toward the barn, feeling more confident that his suspicions were valid. *Where else would they be, at this time of day?* he wondered. It didn't seem likely they were still in town, with the curfew in effect, and there weren't any reasons to be visiting anyone overnight, especially without leaving someone to watch over their stock.

He began to walk with a spring in his step, and he hardly noticed the hunger that gnawed at his stomach, or the grinding pain of his gout. He fantasized about meeting with the local Waffen-SS head, who would be so appreciative that he'd return the family farm to Sverre, or perhaps put him in charge of one of the paper mills out by the Åsenfjord. He envisioned himself wearing a new suit, and moving out of that louse-filled boarding house behind the train station; he imagined twirling out a fat stack of money from his pockets and paying for plates of fist-sized meatballs with gravy and red whortleberries at the Vertshuset Tavern in Trondheim, following them with a bottle of single-malt scotch and a fat cigar.

Sverre confidently approached the barn. Once he reached it, he looked inside, but all he saw were sheep. He slid open the door, and a few lambs squeezed through the slats of the holding pen and approached him, nosing at his pockets for food. The rest of the sheep clustered in their pens and bleated at him, restless and hungry, and behind them, the horse stalls were empty. There was no sign of the pilot anywhere.

His spirits sank, and his fantasy came crashing to a halt. He turned and left the barn, shooing the lambs out of his way and closing the door behind him. *Had he just imagined seeing Erling?* he wondered. He quickly shook the thought from his mind and made his way around to the other side of the barn, nearly falling over when he spotted a rectangular, cart-shaped patch of earth, covered only by the recent snowfall. A set of hoof prints led away from the patch, followed by a pair of deep wheel tracks, which Sverre assumed had been made by a cart.

Following the tracks were a smaller pair of hoof prints, which looked like they belonged to a mule.

CHAPTER 9

An icy mixture of sleet and hail fell in gobs and spatters. The bitter winds made it come sideways and slanting, roundabout and indirect. It was colder than snow and stung like buckshot when it hit the skin, and it lacquered the world with a transparent layer, hardening to ice as the sun set.

Kari and Lance picked up the road on the other side of the river and followed it for a while, riding double through an open valley. Lance sat in front, casually holding Torden's reins. Kari sat behind him with her arms around his waist, shivering in her wet clothes. She buried her face in the back of his coat, breathing in the rich scents of his cigarettes, hair wax, and sweat.

They soon left the valley and made their way into the

hills. In the distance, they could see snow on the blue mountain ranges to the north. To the east, there were even more white-capped mountains, a long line of them stretching as far as the eye could see. The horizon looked like the open mouth of a shark, with row upon row of jagged white peaks.

After riding through the forest for a while, they left the road and pushed Torden up a hill. Kari had to hold on tightly as they ascended, and she could feel Lance's taut muscles through the coat. Her heartbeat accelerated, and in the quiet of the forest, she became aware of the sound of her own breathing. She noticed her father's scent in the coat as well, and she felt guilty for a moment, but she quickly shook the thought from her mind as they continued on their way.

They soon crested the hill and made their way toward a small clearing. Lance glanced behind him as they reached it and saw that it couldn't be seen from the road. He pulled up on the reins and dismounted, then helped Kari down from the horse. Without having him to hold onto, the cold finally caught up to her, and her teeth chattered so much that she could taste the enamel.

Lance tied the horse to a nearby tree and cleared a section of snow from the frozen earth. Then he built a crude fireplace out of rocks and stones. He gathered some birch bark and pine needles from the surrounding area, cut them into tinder, and covered them with broken branches. Then he lit it with his Zippo and took a step back, watching as the small flames spread and took hold in the frozen wood.

Kari walked stiff-legged toward the fire and stood as close to it as she could without burning herself. Without saying a word, Lance went into the forest to gather more wood. He came back after a moment with an armful of snow-crusted logs, the driest-looking of which he carefully placed in the center of the fire. He stacked the rest of them next to the ring of stones before nodding toward Kari's wet clothes.

"Better get out of those before you catch cold," he said.

She hesitated, part of her wanting to, but another part of her afraid. Sensing her uncertainty, he continued.

"Don't worry," he said. "I'm a gentleman."

Before she could reply, he turned his back to her, then cut a green branch from a tree and began to scrape off its bark with his knife. After a long moment, she started to remove her clothing. She took off her jacket, then her sweater, and then her boots and trousers, hanging them by the fire to dry. She hesitated for another moment before removing her long underwear as well, struggling to do so with trembling fingers.

Kari slowly approached the fire, holding her hands out in front of her to warm them but also to be ready to cover herself if Lance turned around. Naked, in the fading dusk light, she was so pale that she almost seemed invisible, blending into the snow. Her heart thudded in her chest, and it became difficult for her to breathe. She'd never been naked in front of a man, least of all a handsome American pilot, and it felt both terrifying and exhilarating. Goose bumps spread across her stomach and limbs, and a warm, queasy feeling grew at the pit of her stomach.

After a moment, Lance spoke without turning around, his words startling her.

"That was quite a show back there," he said. "I don't know if I'd have risked my neck for a horse."

"We've had him since I was a kid," she replied, out of instinct.

"*We?*"

She inwardly cursed herself, realizing her mistake.

"I mean, the people in the valley," she said, her voice wavering. "My family used to borrow him every now and then. We didn't have our own."

"Where's your family now?" he asked.

She hesitated.

"I'm sorry," he said. "I shouldn't have asked—"

She interrupted him.

"It's all right," she said.

"Sometimes I forget there's a war going on," he said.

She didn't reply, and an awkward silence passed. She felt bad for lying to him, even if only by omission, but she knew he wouldn't be with her if she'd been telling him the truth. The silence soon became unbearable, so she finally broke it.

"What about you?" she said.

"What about me what?"

"You have a family?"

He nodded.

"Five sisters and a brother," he said. "My old man was good at making kids, just not so good at sticking around to raise them."

Unable to think of a more subtle way to ask the question she'd wanted to ask since she'd first encountered him, she finally just blurted it out.

"Who's Rozzie Beth?" she asked.

"Beg your pardon?"

"The name on your plane."

He laughed.

"What's so funny?" she said.

"Rozzie Beth's my mother," he said. "Rosalyn Elizabeth Mahurin."

Kari said nothing, embarrassed.

"You thought that was the name of my girl or something, didn't you?" he said.

"No—"

He interrupted her.

"I had a girl back home, but you know how things happen," he said, grinning, before beginning to sing. *"Now I ain't got nobody, and nobody cares for me…"*

She couldn't help but laugh. After a moment, he began to laugh as well. She felt warm, excited, and alive. She wanted to step across the fire and spin him around, and to pull his face to hers and kiss him deeply on the mouth. He surely had to be a better kisser than Håkon or Jan Petter. *But what if he stopped me?* she wondered. *What if he wasn't interested?* She shuddered; the embarrassment and shame would be mortifying.

She hoped he'd make the first move. She closed her eyes and tried to will it to happen, as absurd as that seemed. Before anything did happen, though, she heard something crash through the underbrush nearby. She opened her eyes and looked toward the origin of the sound, covering herself with her hands. Then she heard another crash, followed by some breaking branches.

Torden nickered and tugged at his reins, and Lance stood, drawing his pistol from its holster.

"Wait here," said Lance.

Before Kari could reply, he bolted into the forest with his pistol raised. She grabbed her long underwear and stepped into it, then quickly dressed, pulling on the rest of her still-damp clothing.

Kari removed her knife from its sheath and held it before her, ready to defend herself. After a moment, she heard a gunshot ring out nearby, and her breath caught in her throat.

"Lance?" she said.

He didn't reply. She thought about saying his name again but then stopped herself, realizing that if the Germans had gotten him, she'd be giving herself up as well. She turned and kicked snow on the fire, and it hissed and spat at her before going out. Then she went over and crouched behind a tree, gripping the knife.

After a long, tense moment, Kari saw a shape approaching in the darkness. She tightened her grip on the knife handle, her heart thudding in her chest. For a moment, she thought she saw a man holding a short machine gun, and she stiffened, preparing to strike. Then she relaxed when she realized it was just Lance, holding a rabbit by its haunches.

"I found us some dinner," he said, grinning.

CHAPTER 10

The late afternoon sky lay dark and low, like the ceiling of a longhouse. A pair of hawks circled overhead, searching for prey. Spotting a vole, one of the hawks drifted down and opened its talons to strike. Before it could, though, the animal darted down a tunnel in the snow, and the hawk wheeled back up toward the sky, disappearing behind the clouds.

Erling headed east along the logging roads, avoiding the main road and the towns and villages alongside it. The route meandered, so he rode the mule as hard as he could, trying to cut the distance between Kari and himself. Every time Loki eased up a bit, he snapped the reins or dug his boot heels into Loki's ribs. The mule snorted and whinnied with each jab, but Erling ignored him, driving him onward.

They came to a fork in the road as the sun began to

set, though it was difficult to tell, as the path leading to the east was buried with snow. Erling pulled up on the reins and paused for a moment; he looked to his right, where the logging road curled back toward the main road, and then to his left, where a cluster of farmhouses, including his cousin Reidar's, stood to the north. He wanted to continue heading eastward, and hopefully catch Kari during the night, assuming she'd stop to rest. He knew his animals would need to be looked after, though, and the only one he was comfortable entrusting that to was Reidar, so he nudged his mule toward the path leading north.

They took a waggling trail down through the forest and into a wide, tree-covered valley. Loki's hooves broke through the icy drifts covering the trail and found traction in the underlying snow. As the remaining daylight bled from the sky, the dark trees began to blend with the purpling night. Erling searched for lights in the distance, eventually spotting a burning lamp inside a farmhouse window.

He passed the first pair of farmhouses, leaving the trail and giving them a wide berth in case there were dogs. The last thing he wanted to do was attract attention, as it would have been unusual enough to be travelling out after curfew, much less saddleless upon the back of a mule. Before long, he spotted Reidar's clapboard barn in the distance, looking much larger than he'd remembered. The farmhouse had a fresh coat of mustard-colored paint, and an ornately carved *stabbur* stood between the farmhouse and the barn.

Erling pulled up on Loki's reins and hesitated for a moment, watching a pillar of smoke rise from the farmhouse chimney. He and Reidar had been close growing up—their fathers were brothers—and Reidar had looked up to Erling, as Erling was two years older than him. They'd helped out at each other's farms every summer, and they'd hunted deer together every fall. Erling had even served as the best man at Reidar's wedding, but as Reidar's farm had prospered and his family had grown, Erling's fortunes had gone in the opposite direction. Reidar had tried to help Erling the same way that Erling had helped him, but Erling had stubbornly refused it, and they'd grown apart. He didn't want to ask for Reidar's help now, either, but he couldn't see any other way.

After a long moment, Erling finally got down off his mule and tied him to a nearby tree, not wanting to explain more than he had to to his cousin. Then he set out for Reidar's house, trudging his way through the icy, knee-deep snow. As he approached the farmhouse, he caught a whiff of something gamy and rich cooking inside—his favorite *lapskaus*, perhaps, or maybe *fårikål*—and his stomach rumbled. He pushed the thoughts of food from his mind as he continued on, soon reaching the front door.

Erling turned around and looked to see if Loki could be spotted from the house. After making sure the mule wasn't visible, he turned back toward the door and took a deep breath. Then he knocked. A moment later, he heard muffled voices inside, followed by the sounds of approaching footsteps. The door opened to reveal two burly teenage boys who stood a full head above Erling; the last time he'd seen them, they'd barely reached his waist. Nearby, in the living room, two girls played a game of *Gnav* with their mother, Aase, who looked like she hadn't aged since Erling had last seen her, her hourglass figure impossible to ignore even when blunted by a drab farmwoman's dress.

"Yes?" said the taller boy.

"Erik?" replied Erling, guessing.

The other boy responded.

"Who are you?" he said, narrowing his gaze.

"I'm a cousin of your father's," said Erling.

Before either of the boys could reply, a deep voice bellowed from the next room.

"Who is it?"

Erling turned to see Reidar approaching, wiping his hands on a towel. Reidar had put on weight since Erling had last seen him—he'd never been small, but he looked like the *Julenisse* now, ruddy and plump—and his once-red beard was shot through with streaks of grey. Despite the obvious signs of aging, though, he still had the creaseless brow of a man content with his fate. His sparkling blue eyes widened when he saw his cousin standing in the doorway.

"Erling?"

The way he said it, it sounded more like a question than a statement.

CHAPTER 11

The new day dawned grayer than the previous one. The air smelled like rock salt and sheared metal, and it was cold again, February cold, like the calendar had changed directions and was heading in reverse. To the northwest, by Trondheim, a thin rope of black smoke rose twisting in the wind. To the south, thick storm clouds gathered over the mountains, pooling like spilled mercury. It felt ominous and still, like the world was coming to an end.

It was still dark when Kari woke. She'd only slept a few hours, despite being exhausted. Birdsong and other morning noises had pulled her from a dreamless sleep, and shivering, she instinctively reached for her blankets. When her hands found her trousers instead, and the cold, hard ground beneath her, she bolted upright, suddenly remembering where she was.

She wiped the sleep from her eyes and glanced around at her surroundings. The fire lay in its ashes, a ring of matted, dead grass around it where the snow had melted. Lance lay across from her with his hands between his legs, curled up like a pill bug. He looked boyish as he slept, his brow slack and the lines gone from his face.

Kari watched Lance for a while as the sun climbed behind him, over the eastern mountains. She wondered what he'd done before he'd become a pilot. *Had he gone to college, or was he a tradesman or a farmer, like her father? Was he from the south, which she knew nothing about, other than what she'd seen in* Gone With The Wind, *or was he from the west? Maybe California, or Texas?* She thought about the other woman he'd mentioned, and wondered if she'd been pretty, or smart, or easy, like the girls from Trondheim who wore makeup and made fun of her plain clothing. *Would he see more in her than he'd seen in his last girlfriend, or would he be joking about her with the next woman he'd meet, referring to her as some simple farm girl he'd taken advantage of in order to get home?* Then she thought about her father, alone at their farm. She suddenly felt guilty again, and then she felt angry with Erling for having the power to make her feel that way.

She continued to watch Lance until the sun had risen above the mountains, and the rats and other nocturnal animals had returned to their nests and dens. After a while, the trilling music of a swallow finally pulled him from his sleep. He opened his eyes and glanced around, his gaze narrowing as it stopped on her.

"How long have you been watching me?" he asked.

"Not long," she said.

He grinned. She fought the urge to smile back, turning away.

A black dot appeared on the horizon, above the mountains east of Hegra. After a moment, another point appeared, and then a third spot that was larger than the other two. Outlines soon emerged as the approaching shapes swelled in size; they first looked like insects, and then birds, and finally, German warplanes. A deep droning noise accompanied them, growing louder as the aircraft approached and pushing aside the quiet of the cold winter morning. The planes flashed overhead with a thunderous roar, and just as quickly as they'd appeared, they began to disappear again, growing smaller and smaller as they faded into the distance.

Moltke and his men rode the half-tracks toward the farm closest to the crash site. He sat in the back of the trailing vehicle and sipped whiskey-laced coffee from his silver flask, trying to still a headache that made his skull feel like it was in a vise. They'd spent the night in Hegra, at a hotel the Waffen-SS had taken over during their siege against the nearby fortress. As much as he'd disliked Trondheim, Moltke had found his backcountry accommodations even worse. After eating a flavorless meal of boiled potatoes, boiled cauliflower, and boiled whitefish, he'd been forced to share a room with one of his men, sleeping on a lumpy mattress that smelled of mothballs and hay. Half the night, he'd stared at the water-stained ceiling thinking about how far away Africa was, while the other half he'd spent trying to ignore the sounds of Schweitzer in the next room, rutting with the hotel maid.

The half-tracks soon crested a hill and barreled down a cratered dirt road, causing Moltke to taste bile at the back of his throat. He chased it with another swig of his whiskey-laced coffee—which contained too much weak Norwegian coffee and not enough Irish whiskey for his tastes—and then he put away the flask, not wanting to run out before the day wasn't even halfway through. Then he looked ahead and saw the farmhouse in the distance, where a young child carried a pair of tin pails toward a crumbling barn. He frowned as he lit a cigarette, noting that it looked more like something out of a Caspar David Friedrich painting than an actual war.

They pulled the half-tracks to a stop at the end of the road, then got out and approached the barn. Goetz had polished Moltke's riding boots that morning, and Moltke had worn the *Totenkopf* insignia on his collar and hatband patches, hoping it would instill fear in the locals. A burly farmer emerged from the barn before they got there and stared blankly at the men, his bloodshot eyes glassed over.

Moltke took a small notebook from the pocket of his trench coat and checked the background information he'd gotten from the Gestapo—the farmer's name was Gustav Lorck; he came from a long line of smallholders; he had a wife and five children, he'd surrendered his firearms when he'd been ordered to, and he had no apparent ties to the resistance.

"Herr Lorck?" said Moltke.

The farmer narrowed his gaze, but he said nothing.

"*Sprechen Sie Deutsch?*"

The farmer shook his head.

"How about English?" asked Moltke. "*Snakker du engelsk?*"

Again, the farmer shook his head. Moltke turned to Schweitzer.

"Ask him about the pilot," he said.

Schweitzer addressed the farmer in clunky Norwegian. The farmer replied in Norwegian, keeping his eyes on Moltke.

"What'd he say?" asked Moltke.

"He says he doesn't know anything about any pilot," said Schweitzer.

Moltke looked into the barn and saw two young children milking a pair of thin cows.

"Where are his other children?" said Moltke.

Schweitzer addressed the farmer in Norwegian again, and the farmer replied again in Norwegian, shaking his head.

"Well?" said Moltke.

"He said he doesn't have any other children," said Schweitzer.

"He's lying," said Moltke, pointing to his black book. "It says here he has five children. Where are the others?"

Schweitzer addressed the farmer in Norwegian, and the farmer replied, shaking his head and growing upset.

"He says you're mistaken," said Schweitzer.

Moltke turned to the others.

"Search the house," he said.

Blücher and two of the enlisted men approached the house, their machine guns raised. The farmer went after them and grabbed Blücher by the arm, spinning him around. Blücher pointed his machine gun at the farmer's chest, and Moltke's heart leapt into his throat.

"*Loslassen!*" shouted Blücher.

Ignoring him, the farmer grabbed Blücher's machine gun by the barrel and pointed it toward the sky.

"*Stehen bleiben,*" said Moltke.

The farmer ignored him, and he and Blücher wrestled for control of the machine gun as the others looked on.

"*Stehen bleiben!*" shouted Moltke, his voice wavering.

The farmer continued to fight with Blücher, gaining control of the machine gun and turning it on Blücher, but Schweitzer pulled out his Browning pistol and pointed it at the farmer's head before the farmer could pull the trigger.

"Lower the gun," said Schweitzer, first in English and

then in Norwegian. Defiant, the farmer hesitated.
Schweitzer cocked the hammer of his pistol and repeated
his command, but before the farmer could react, a child
spoke from the barn.

"Wait," said the child.

They all turned to see a nine-year old girl standing at
the entrance to the barn.

"I speak some English," said the girl. "I learn at
school, before the war."

"Where are the others?" said Moltke, his heart
hammering in his chest.

The farmer continued to shout at them in Norwegian,
and Moltke turned to his men.

"Shut him up," he said.

Goetz and Schweitzer grabbed the farmer and took
the machine gun from him. The farmer started to speak,
but before he could finish, Schweitzer smacked him in the
mouth.

"*Halt die Klappe!*" said Schweitzer.

Moltke turned back to the girl.

"Where are they?" he said.

"I show you," she said.

Moltke hesitated.

"Come," said the girl, beckoning with her tiny hand.
"It's okay."

After a moment, Moltke turned to his men and
nodded to the farmer.

"Watch him," he said to Schweitzer.

Schweitzer put his pistol to the farmer's head and shoved him forward while Moltke and the others followed the girl into the forest. They wandered along a narrow and curling path through the wilderness, past an old *stabbur* that had caved in upon itself. For some reason, Moltke thought of the Grimms' fairy tale *The Wolf and the Fox*, and how the smaller fox had tricked the wolf, leading to the wolf's demise. He pulled his Walther P38 from its holster and held it by his side as he continued on, his finger hovering above the trigger.

They crossed a frozen creek and went up and then down a small hill. Then the girl led them to a clearing. Three small, knee-high mounds stood in the snow before them, lined in a row. A larger mound stood behind them, underneath a copse of crooked trees.

The girl knelt down next to one of the smaller mounds and began to clear away the snow, but Moltke ordered his men to stop her. Then he turned to Goetz and nodded, and Goetz kneeled down where the girl had been and finished clearing away the snow, revealing a small headstone with the name "MARTIN" on it, above a cross and the dates 1935-1942. Goetz cleared the snow off the next mound, revealing the name "BERIT" above another cross and the dates 1932-1942, and then cleared the snow from the last, which had the name "ELSE" above a tiny cross, over the dates 1939-1942.

"They got sick," said the girl. "*Tuberkulose.*"

The farmer continued to rail at them in Norwegian,

tears streaming down his reddening cheeks. Moltke
turned away and looked toward the mountains, his
thudding heart finally slowing down in his chest, though
his stomach was once again beginning to roil.

A light snow fell in the late morning. It lasted just minutes,
and it left little more than a dusting atop the previous
snowfall. Still, it felt like the clouds were somehow trying
to remind them of their authority, and they remained
firmly overhead, a swollen grey belly fixed to the bottom
of the sky.

Moltke and his men rode the half-tracks toward
another farm in the Stjørdalen Valley. Along the way, he
looked to his notebook again and checked the information
the Gestapo had given him. According to the notes, a man
named Birger Tørrisen lived at the next farm with his wife
and two teenage daughters. His wife was a cousin of the
Quisling mayor of Trondheim who the Germans had put
into power in 1941; Birger had been flagged for being part
of the Trøndelag Teater when he was a student at the
Norwegian College of Teaching in the early 1920s, but
he'd done nothing suspicious since then, and he wasn't
being monitored. The outdated information that Moltke
had gotten on the Lorck family had been an exception;
aside from that, the Gestapo's information on the residents
of the valley had been thorough and up-to-date, thanks to
their network of spies and Quisling informers.

Moltke put away his notebook and took out his flask, but when he went to drink from it, he realized it was empty. He inwardly cursed himself for finishing it so quickly, wishing he'd brought more, or had at least better paced himself. His mouth was as dry as cotton, and his headache had slowly transitioned from a dull to a throbbing pain, punctuated by every bump in the road or loud noise. He knew that Goetz carried a flask of *korn* with him, but he couldn't stand the smell of the cheap liquor much less the idea of drinking from the same bottle as Goetz. He refilled his flask with water instead and kept to his cigarettes, smoking one after another despite the raw feeling they left in his throat.

They soon turned onto a road buried with unspoiled snow and followed it toward a large red farmhouse. Before they even pulled to a stop, Moltke could tell that no one had been there in days; the snow around the house and barn was untouched, and no smoke rose from the farmhouse's chimney. Perhaps the Tørrisens were in Trondheim, he assumed, visiting family; according to the Gestapo's information, Birger's brother was a civil servant there, and their mother resided at a sanatorium.

They pulled the half-tracks to a stop and got out, and Moltke turned to his men.

"Check the house and the barn," he said. Then he lit another cigarette, took a deep drag, and closed his eyes. He imagined his grandfather, seated atop his cavalry horse, leading his men during the Austro-Prussian War's decisive Battle of Königgrätz. Then he pictured his father, saber in hand, turning away an Allied charge on Çanak Bayırı at Gallipoli. He imagined the embarrassed and ashamed expressions on their faces, if they could see him now, going from farm to farm in rural Norway, looking for a downed and probably unarmed pilot. He envisioned his overweight wife Gertrud and their spoiled daughters Ursula and Frauke, whom he hadn't seen in eight months but who didn't seem to miss him, only sending a few perfunctory letters during that time. He shook their disappointed faces from his mind and thought of Elise instead, lying naked on the divan in her uncle's Berlin apartment, her hands clasped behind her head and a look in her eyes that was both confident and unashamed. *If only I could go back to that moment and do things differently*, he thought to himself.

Before long, Blücher's oafish voice broke Moltke's reverie.

"Herr Oberleutnant."

Moltke opened his eyes and spotted a skinny, bearded man in an overcoat approaching on a rusty bicycle, pedaling like a maniac and slipping and sliding through the snow.

"*Was zum Teufel…?*" said Goetz.

Moltke turned to Schweitzer, who raised his rifle and aimed it at the man on the bicycle.

"Fire a warning shot," said Moltke.

Schweitzer raised the rifle a few centimeters, then

squeezed the trigger and fired a shot over the man's head. The man swerved off the road and crashed his bicycle into a snowdrift, going over his handlebars. After landing face-first in the snow, he scrambled to his feet and came running toward them with his hands in the air.

"Don't shoot!" shouted the man, in clumsy German. "I'm unarmed."

CHAPTER 12

A mizzling sleet began to fall, varnishing the world with a another coat of ice. In the distance, the mountaintops disappeared beneath a grey smother of gathering storm clouds. The birds left the darkening sky to hide in their nests or in the evergreens, and the world grew quiet again without their twittering song.

Erling slept astride the mule. He'd drifted off at some point during the morning after riding all night without rest. He faded in and out of a tenuous sleep, his grasp on time and space wavering as his dreams mingled with reality. One moment, he was riding Loki back at their farm, pulling a plough over a barren field; the next moment, he was back in the present, chasing Kari toward the Swedish border, and the moment after that, he was dreaming again, riding across the Stjørdalen Valley as a young man to see Martha at her grandparents' farm.

He shook his head and slapped himself, but it didn't help. He soon faded off again, dreaming of *Njal*-marked fjord horses pulling felled timber to the river, their hooves booming like thunder. Loki clambered onward through the spruce-choked hills, breaking thin plates of ice where the snow had melted and then frozen again. Going down an incline, Erling pitched forward when Loki slipped on some rocks, and he smashed his face against the mule's neck, bloodying his nose.

He sawed back hard on the reins, jerking Loki to a stop. Erling dismounted the mule and made his way to a nearby stream, where he dunked his head into the frigid water. It felt like cold fire, but he stayed under as long as he could. Then he surfaced again, gasping for air as the blood rushed to his face.

Erling bent down and drank as much of the icy water as he could bear, getting rid of the coppery taste in his mouth. Then he made his way back toward the mule, his heart pounding in his chest. He noticed that Loki was favoring his left hind leg, then saw blood speckling their tracks. He knelt down and examined Loki's hoof, finding a deep crack slicing across it.

He led Loki to the creek and washed away the dirt and blood from Loki's injured hoof, whispering old *Bånsuller* to the skittish mule. Loki recoiled from the frigid water, but the pain of the cold dulled the pain of the injury, and he soon quit resisting. Erling unsheathed his knife and scraped Loki's hoof clean, then went about lacing the crack. After he finished, he patched it with thick sap from a nearby spruce tree, then cut off a strip of his long underwear and tied a makeshift bandage over the hoof.

Erling washed the knife in the creek, then plunged his head once more into the icy water. He walked back over to Loki and fed him the rest of the oats he'd bought in Hegra, even though he was starving and would've preferred to have eaten them himself. He considered eating the last strip of jerky he had but then decided against it. Then he mounted the mule and rode onward, taking the twisting road east through the spruce-choked forest.

He crossed through the low country of the valley and rode the crakes and dabchicks up out of the frozen marshes. Then he followed the trail up toward the mountains, past a section of recently cleared forest. The trail branched and broke along a series of low hills, and losing his sense of direction, Erling looked toward the sky for the sun to guide him. When he finally located it overhead, glinting like a piece of topaz beneath ice, he tugged at the reins and nudged the mule onward toward another valley to the southeast.

Before long, he spotted the remains of the Hegra Bridge, lying in an ice dam choking the Stjørdal River. He pulled up on the reins and brought the mule to a halt, then looked downriver for a narrow point to cross. Finding none, he glanced upriver. He nearly exploded with rage when his eyes stopped on a cart submerged in the ice dam—his cart, as he recognized its misshapen tailboard and the splinter bar that he'd fashioned himself. Then he suddenly felt sick, realizing that Kari might be underneath the ice along with it.

Erling jumped off the mule and ran down to the water. He scrambled out onto the ice, slipping and sliding his way across the craggy mess. The freeze-up strained and cracked as he crossed it, but he ignored the sounds, searching desperately for his daughter. If she were indeed down in that icy black water, he'd never forgive himself for initially thinking of his cart.

Erling checked the area around the cart, but he found nothing. He widened his search, getting down on his hands and knees and straining to see past the milky crumble. He still saw nothing below, and his heart sank at the prospect of losing Kari. Then he spotted a crooked shape beneath the ice that looked like an arm, or perhaps a leg.

He pounded against the ice with his fist, but it wouldn't break. He stood up and stomped on it, and it creaked a bit but still held. Erling looked toward the shore and saw a large rock jutting up from the snow. He ran over toward the riverbank and pried the rock free, then carried it back onto the ice.

He raised the rock over his head and smashed it down onto the ice as hard as he could. The impact sounded like a thunderclap, but it barely made a dent. He raised the rock and smashed it down again and again, putting everything he had into it. The ice finally began to break up, and the whacks grew slushy as the freed water seeped up from beneath.

He tossed aside the rock and plunged his arm into the icy water. It was so cold that it took his breath away, but he ignored the pain and moved his arm around, searching for the limb. His arm thickened in the freezing water, growing numb and slow, so he pulled it out and reached down with the other arm. His fingertips soon found something soft and giving, and he tugged at it, but it came loose. He reached again and grabbed the object, but before he even pulled it to the surface, he knew by its weight and feel that it was only a log.

Erling scoured the ice again for signs of Kari, but he found nothing. Then he looked toward the bank on the other side of the river, and he saw a violent scrawl of hoof prints leading up onto solid ground. He scrambled to his feet and hurried over to the riverbank, searching the snowdrifts for tracks. He soon found a large pair of boot prints leading off into the wilderness.

Not far from away them and heading in the same direction were a smaller set of footprints, which appeared to be Kari's size.

CHAPTER 13

The temperature dropped as the day progressed, and the sleet transformed to snow. It came down fine at first, falling like powdered sugar. Then it fell thick and heavy, burying the world once again with silence.

Kari and Lance rode all morning and into the early afternoon. She sat out in front, holding the reins; he sat in back, clinging to her whenever the trail became rough. Some time after they'd crossed the Trøbekken stream, he'd fallen asleep, leaning forward and burying his face into her shoulder. She could feel his breath against her neck and his stubble against her skin, and it sent warm shivers up her spine.

She carefully steered the horse around the ditches and ice patches in their path, hoping to prolong the time he spent sleeping upon her shoulder. After a while, she peered over and saw the side of his head, noticing a small scar on his scalp, just behind his left ear. She wondered what it had been from—*was it from shrapnel or a crash, or was it from his childhood, falling off a bicycle or getting into a fight?* She closed her eyes and breathed in the rich, beeswax scent of his Brylcream, imagining lying next to him on a reindeer hide in front of a warm fire.

The sound of the wind shaking the trees roused Kari from her daydream, and after a few moments, Lance woke as well, licking his dry lips as he glanced around and got his bearings. They rode Torden up a knuckled ridge and then down into a valley, where they soon picked up the old logging road. Kari snapped at the reins, and Torden picked up his speed, cutting a broken path through the virgin snow.

They continued along the buried road, not seeing a single mark of mankind all day other than the faint outline of the road they followed. Mists moved all around them like fleeing deer; above the treetops, the mountains to the north looked distant and blurry in the wet air, like smudges of purple and blue paint, and the light from the sky fell milky and grey, lingering on the afternoon.

After a while, they saw a set of tire tracks in the road before them, spinning out in a sloppy arc and heading back in the direction they'd come from. At first, it had seemed like a mistake, but then they saw a second set of tracks, and then a third, wider set that looked like they belonged to a half-track or even an armored tank. Before long, the road was crisscrossed with tracks, multiplying and becoming fresher the further they went. It reminded Kari of the spider webs she used to find in their barn, all zigzagging patchworks of angles and lines.

They left the road and tied Torden to a tree. Then they continued on through the forest on foot, avoiding open spaces and moving as quietly as possible. The snow was crusty underfoot, and the cold air had a cruel bite. They slowly made their way through the thick forest, then up another ridge and around a tangle of hedges blocking their way.

They eventually emerged from the forest and spotted the village of Meråker in the distance, at the bottom of a valley. The first thing Kari saw was the crucifix-shaped wind vane atop the old Meråker church. Then she saw the long, red railway station, and just beyond it, a few dozen houses carved into the sloping hillside.

They pushed forward toward the edge of the tree line to get a better view. Once they reached it, Kari could see a number of German vehicles parked outside the train station, painted in Wehrmacht *dunkelgrau* and blending into the landscape. She could also see eight more Waffen-SS, anonymous beneath their black, scuttle-shaped helmets.

"Why are there so many Krauts here?" asked Lance.

"I don't know," said Kari.

They watched as another half-track pulled up to the

station. After it stopped, six more soldiers got out and joined the others. Kari turned back to Lance.

"I'll go find out what's going on," she said, starting for the village.

Lance grabbed her arm.

"Wait," he said. "I'll go."

"You can't," she said. "If they see you, they'll kill you."

Lance hesitated, knowing that she had a point. He pulled out his pistol and offered it to her.

"Take this," he said.

"Keep it."

"You sure?"

She nodded.

"They're not looking for me," she said, then turned and set out. She could feel his eyes on her as she walked off through the forest. She wanted to turn around and smile, but she didn't want him to see how nervous she was, so she continued on without looking back.

Kari walked through the forest and down into the vale, slipping and sliding along an uneven decline. She tripped a few times along the way, barking her shins and stubbing her pinky toes. At the bottom of the hill, the terrain leveled again, and the forest thinned out. She hid behind the trees as long as she could, and when there was no more forest to shelter her, she went out into the open and made her way toward a dirt road.

She followed the road past a sod-covered house and

slowed her pace as she approached the outskirts of the village. She'd been to Meråker a few times as a girl, on her way to Sweden; it was larger than Hegra, and the houses were larger, too, and nicer than the ones in the Stjørdalen Valley, with slate roofs and fresh coats of paint, thanks to the money from the local mining industry.

Kari passed the elementary school, which had already closed for the day. Then she approached the center of town. The village's utility poles had been painted with white bands, presumably for blackouts; the few street lamps had been painted black, too, except for a thin slit. There weren't many locals out, and the few that were minded their own business, avoiding eye contact. After she passed Meråker *Handelsforening*, the large market and center of the town, Kari noticed someone watching her from the second-story window of a house. Unnerved, she lowered her head and continued on her way.

She soon spotted a poster affixed to a pole, written in German, the words in bold red lettering. *Achtung!*, it began. *Reisende Wehrmachtangehörige! Der Fiend ist überall!* Her German wasn't perfect, but she understood the gist of it. *Attention! German military travelers! The enemy is everywhere!* Was it legitimate, she wondered, or was it the work of the Norwegian resistance? It was impossible to tell.

She continued her way through the village. Before long, she spotted the church, atop a cleared hill. A few dozen black crosses stood half-buried in the snow, sticking up like cloves in an Easter ham, and a light burned inside one of the windows.

Kari turned and set out for the church, then hesitated. She'd occasionally attended services as a child, sitting impatiently on the hard wooden pews while the preachers gave sermons about vague subjects like submission and mercy. She'd gone to Sunday school with the other girls from the valley, and she'd mastered Luther's Small Catechism and all the important hymns. She'd never felt anything from religion, though, and after God hadn't answered her prayers to save her dying mother, she'd stopped making an effort.

She decided against seeking help there and continued on her way. After rounding a bend in the road, Kari spotted a young man behind the tavern, smoking a cigarette. She slowed her pace and considered asking him about the German presence, then hesitated, unsure. Perhaps it was the way he seemed so at ease while everyone else seemed on edge, or the way his probing glance bored through her when their eyes met. She decided to avoid him as well, continuing on and heading toward the other side of town.

After reaching an intersection, she turned onto a one-lane road running alongside the Stjørdal River. Then she noticed a sign for the Meråker smelting plant. She suddenly realized that the Germans must be there to protect it. In February, she'd heard on a classmate's contraband radio about the sabotage at the heavy water plant in Vemork. The Germans must have been increasing security as a result of that, she assumed, which meant they were probably protecting the rest of the plants, dams, and train stations between there and the Swedish border as well.

Kari turned onto the road and made her way back across Meråker. She plotted their new route in her mind, figuring their best chance at getting to Sweden was across the highland trails she used to take with her father, when they went to Åre and Järpen in the summer to sell their wool. It wasn't an easy route, but the only Germans that might be up there were the *Gebirgsjäger*, the mountain infantry units that hunted the Norwegian resistance and the Inter-Allied Commandos. She considered stopping at the *Handelsforening* on her way back to buy provisions with their remaining money, knowing they'd need them if they headed into the highlands. Approaching it, though, she saw at least a dozen Waffen-SS outside, so she passed by without stopping.

She picked up her pace. Seeing a compost heap behind a house, she went over and looked through it, but the stench made her gag, and there was nothing worth taking. She kept going and then stopped and checked the compost heap outside the next house. She grabbed a few moldy potatoes off the pile, then continued on her way.

Kari soon left the dirt road and followed her slowly vanishing trail back through the forest. She used the sheath knife to cut the moldy parts off the potatoes while contemplating their new route. Though they weren't likely to run into anyone, the highland trails were a much more difficult route than the logging roads. One benefit, though, was that it would take longer to get to Sweden, which meant that she'd have more time with Lance.

She returned to the hill and struggled her way up the rocky incline, falling halfway up the slope and sliding back down to the bottom of it. She tried again and again, and on her fourth attempt, she finally reached the top. Then she made her way through the forest back to the clearing where she'd left Lance.

She brushed the snow off her coat and pants, then smoothed back her hair, wanting to look her best. Before long, she saw the copse of trees where Lance had been waiting, but he wasn't anywhere to be seen. She rushed over to the clearing and saw a few sets of fresh footprints in the snow. One pair she recognized as Lance's, but the other two didn't belong to him. They were larger, and the spacing was different. *Did they belong to Norwegians or Germans?* she wondered. It was impossible to tell.

Kari rushed back to the tree where they'd left Torden, only to find him missing as well. Lance's footprints headed off into the forest from there, along with Torden's hoof prints. The other two sets of footprints also proceeded in the same direction.

A queasy feeling rose in Kari's stomach, and she felt her chest tightening as she followed the trail. *What if he'd been caught?* she wondered. *Or worse... what if he'd left her?*

What if he'd found the resistance, or they'd found him, and they'd offered to take him to Sweden themselves? She tried to count to five with each inhale and each exhale, struggling to keep from hyperventilating.

She continued to follow the tracks until they abruptly stopped. The larger two sets of footprints switched back and headed off in another direction. Lance's trail, however, came to an end; it looked like both he and Torden had disappeared. *How could that be possible?* she wondered. *Had they carried him away?* She searched for signs of where they might have gone, but there was nothing to be found.

Kari began to panic again. She broadened her search, scouring the area in ever-widening circles. She eventually spotted some faint tracks behind a stand of trees; they looked like they'd been smoothed over with a pine branch, or perhaps a coat.

Kari followed the tracks, her sense of dread quickly replaced by a flicker of hope. The tracks eventually became sharper again, and a pair of hoof prints emerged from the snow. Not long after that, she made out Lance's distinct boot prints as well.

She continued on through the forest. Her heart stopped when she heard a whistle in the distance. She scanned the area, spotting Lance in a thick stand of evergreens. He held Torden's reins, and the horse stood behind him, ducking his head beneath the low-hanging branches.

Kari approached Lance.

"What happened?" she asked.

"Two men came up here, with rifles," he said. "I don't know if they were Germans or not, but I wasn't about to find out."

Before she could reply, they heard the buzz of an engine in the distance. Kari grabbed Torden's reins, and without saying another word, they hurried off into the forest.

CHAPTER 14

The wind rose howling off the mountaintops and stirred the clouds, breaking them up into wispy strands of cirrus. Small patches of blue gradually emerged between them, the first streaks of color the sky had shown in days. They didn't last long, though; as soon as the late afternoon sun dipped toward the west, the blue patches faded to a matte purple and then back to a lusterless black.

Moltke looked up at the shifting clouds as he and his men rode out toward the Dahlstrøm farm. He saw the vague shape of a horse's head among them, its open mouth braying at some unseen provocation. The winds fanned and stretched it out into the shape of a crude sickle, and then a pair of bones, and then, finally, nothing. He thought back to the *Internationaler Wolkenatlas* he'd seen while a student at the *Kriegsakademie*; it had seemed like such an indulgence to him at the time, for people to be documenting something so ephemeral as the clouds. Only now after living through his second World War was he beginning to see that their efforts were just as fleeting; the grand sum of all the battles they'd fought and all the borders they'd drawn and redrawn seemed no less transitory than the clouds, and no more tangible, either.

Schweitzer stomped on the brakes, jolting Moltke from his daydream and bringing the half-track to a fishtailing halt. The enlisted men seated in back piled up against those seated near the front, shoving them against seatbacks or to the floor. Moltke, who'd been sitting in the middle, tumbled to the deck, then fought his way back to his feet, cursing and shoving at his men. He looked ahead over the half-track's nose armor and saw the other half-track in front of them, jackknifed into a ditch.

The men jumped out of the half-track and approached the wreck. Thick black smoke poured out from its engine block, and its tank treads whirred through the empty air. One by one, the dazed passengers crawled from the vehicle, cradling injured arms or holding their battered heads. The gangly young driver was the last to emerge, his nose swollen to the size of a lemon and leaking blood.

"*Verdammte Scheiße!*" said Schweitzer, looking over the wreck. "Are you blind?"

The young driver shook his head, dripping blood all

over the front of his uniform.

"Sorry, sir," he mumbled.

"Get it out of there," said Moltke.

Schweitzer climbed behind the wheel and tried to reverse the half-track out of the ditch. It didn't move, its treads chewing up the icy mud and spitting slushy geysers of it into the air. Schweitzer tried again and again, cycling through the gears, but it still wouldn't budge. He climbed out and ordered the other men to help him push it, but it was no use; the half-track was firmly stuck.

"Now what?" said Goetz.

"Destroy it," said Moltke.

Schweitzer approached the wreck. He took a stick grenade from his belt, yanked its cord, and shoved it under the half-track's hood. The men scattered for cover as Schweitzer hurried away from the wreck, and a moment later, the front of the half-track exploded in a thunderous ball of flames.

Moltke turned to Blücher, nodding toward the young driver.

"Take him back to Hegra," he said. Then he turned and addressed the others: "The rest of you, back in the vehicle."

The men grabbed their gear and piled into the remaining half-track. Moltke got in last, taking a seat in back. Schweitzer climbed in behind the wheel and started the engine, and a moment later, they were moving again. A few of the men glanced over their shoulders at Blücher and the young driver, but Moltke didn't look back, keeping his eyes on the road ahead.

They continued their way along the winding country road. Schweitzer slowed the half-track to a crawl, driving in second gear to avoid ditching it. The enlisted men sat shoulder-to-shoulder in the middle of the vehicle, blowing on their hands and stamping their feet to keep warm. Moltke sat alone in back, staring off into the forest and smoking one cigarette after another to quell his headache.

They soon left the country road and turned off onto an old dirt path. Schweitzer dropped the half-track into first gear, and the engine strained as they made their way down a hill. After they rounded a bend in path, Moltke looked ahead and saw a yellow farmhouse in the distance. He checked the Gestapo's file; according to the notes, one of the most valuable informers in the Stjørdalen Valley lived there. The next farm was the one they were looking for; it belonged to a widower named Erling Dahlstrøm, whose daughter Kari had been named as the one helping the downed pilot. They had no apparent ties to the Quislings or the resistance; they were what the Gestapo called *unberechenbar*, or unpredictables, who were to be regarded with scrutiny and caution.

Moltke put away his notebook and took a long drink from his flask, trying to get rid of the vile taste at the back of his throat. The man on the bicycle who'd brought the girl to their attention had repulsed him; it wasn't just his shabby appearance, or his rotten breath or ill manners. It was his ruthless, unabashed opportunism; Moltke had known dozens like him back in Berlin, who'd turn in a lifelong neighbor or co-worker for a better apartment or an extra ration card. It was the only lead they'd gotten, though, and he was glad to have it, despite its source. The sooner they found the pilot, the sooner he could get back to Trondheim, and the sooner he could start working on his transfer papers.

Before long, they rounded another bend in the dirt road. Soon after that, they spotted the Dahlstrøm's crumbling barn in the distance. Schweitzer parked the half-track in between the barn and the run-down farmhouse, and the men got out.

Moltke turned to Goetz and one of the enlisted men.

"Check the barn," he said. Then he followed Schweitzer and the other enlisted man toward the farmhouse.

From a distance, the farmhouse didn't appear occupied; no smoke rose from the stove chimney, and no lights burned inside. There weren't any fresh footprints leading to or away from the house, either; the few that were there had been rounded or concealed by the recent snowfall. It didn't look abandoned, though; despite being shabby, there were plenty of signs of someone living there, including some potato peels atop a compost pile and a stack of recently chopped wood.

Schweitzer nodded to the enlisted man, and the enlisted man knocked on the door. They waited for a moment, but there was no reply. Schweitzer looked in through a window, but he saw no one inside. After another moment, he kicked in the front door and went in with his machine gun raised, and the enlisted man followed him.

Moltke entered the house after his men. Schweitzer and the enlisted man stormed from room to room, checking inside closets and under beds. Moltke went into the living room, which seemed oddly sterile to him; there were no photographs or personal touches anywhere, other than a ratty throw blanket and a simple landscape in a cheap wooden frame.

After examining the living room, Moltke checked the kitchen. He noticed that the cupboards were barren, the stove was cold, and the sink was dry. The bottom of a coffee cup had a black crust on it, and the pail water had a faint, stagnant odor. It seemed like no one had been there for days.

Once he finished searching the kitchen, Moltke went back into the living room, where he met up with the others.

"Did you find anything?" he said.

"Just these," said Schweitzer, showing Moltke the American postcards from Kari's room.

Before Moltke could reply, they heard someone shout his name. They hurried outside, where they saw a horse-drawn cart approaching in the distance, being pulled by a sturdy-looking fjord horse. Reidar sat on the cart, holding the reins; his teenage daughter Hanne sat next to him, her hands hidden beneath a blanket.

Moltke turned to his men.

"Be ready," he said.

The soldiers gripped their machine guns as the cart approached. Before it got within twenty meters of them, Moltke addressed the driver.

"Herr Dahlstrøm?"

Reidar slowly nodded as he pulled up on the reins.

"Do you speak German?" asked Moltke.

"Some," said Reidar.

"Where were you?"

"Bringing a sheep to town."

Moltke nodded toward the house.

"It looks like you've been gone for some time," he said.

"Just the day," said Reidar, his German clunky and slow.

Moltke's gaze narrowed.

"Is there anyone who can confirm that?" he said.

"You can check with the butcher," said Reidar.

"Which one?" said Moltke, opening his notebook.

"There's only one in town," said Reidar. "We stopped at the store, too."

Moltke nodded to Hanne.

"And who are you?"

Reidar responded before she could reply.

"What's this about?"

"I asked the girl a question," said Moltke, turning to her. "You can speak, can't you?"

After a moment, Hanne answered.

"My name's Kari," she said, her voice wavering.

"Where are your papers, Kari?"

Reidar nodded toward the house.

"They're inside," he said.

"You're supposed to have them with you at all times," said Moltke.

Reidar began to climb down from the cart.

"I can get them—"

Moltke interrupted Reidar.

"That's all right," he said, nodding to the girl. "She can go."

Hanne looked to Reidar, uncertain. Reidar nodded, and after a moment, Hanne got down from the cart and approached the house. Reidar watched her go, his heart pounding in his chest. *Goddamn that stubborn Erling*, he thought to himself. *I knew we should've gone to the resistance.* He thought about the rifle he had hidden beneath the seat of his cart, then counted the German soldiers. He figured he could take out two of them, or maybe three if he was lucky, but certainly not five. He looked toward the house, hoping Hanne might flee out one of the back windows. *If she doesn't come back soon*, he thought to himself, *I'm going to have to do something. If I try to take on them all, it's suicide, but if I don't do anything, we'll end up at Falstad, or worse.*

Before Reidar could decide what to do, he heard a

buzzing noise in the distance. He and the others turned toward the origin of the sound, and a moment later, a German soldier appeared on the horizon, approaching on a motorcycle and slipping and sliding in the thick snow.

The men gathered around as the soldier pulled the motorcycle to a stop and cut off the engine. The soldier then addressed Moltke, out of breath.

"Herr Oberleutnant?"

"Yes?"

"We found the body of an Allied pilot nearby," said the soldier. "Near a farm in Lånke."

"Well, what are you waiting for?" said Moltke. "Take us to it."

Without saying another word, Moltke and his men piled back into the half-track and drove off after the motorcycle.

Reidar watched them go. It took a long time for his hands to finally stop trembling.

CHAPTER 15

The mountains fused on the horizon with the bunching storm clouds. The last remaining daylight bled away, leaving behind a limited palette of ever-darkening hues. Edges blurred and shapes grew faint and indistinct, and the world took on a surreal and dreamlike quality. It was once again becoming the dark and shadowy place that inspired stories of trolls and monsters.

Erling rode the balking mule onward through the foothills. The makeshift bandage he'd applied held for a while, but after a few hours, it had become tatters. The exposed crack in Loki's hoof had deepened and grown wider, and the hoof had resumed bleeding. It left an intermittent blood trail in their wake, blemishing the snow.

He massaged the mule's neck and whispered more poems into his ear, including the works of Bjørnstjerne Bjørnson, which he'd memorized as a boy.

I sat and waited through evenings long
and scanned the ridge with the spruces yonder;
but darkening mountains made shadows throng,
and you the way did not wander.

He repeated the poems over and over, but the soothing words didn't help; the injured mule's strength was dwindling, and he began to sag beneath Erling's weight.

They soon emerged from the foothills and descended into a valley. After crossing it, they entered another stretch of forest. Halfway up a hill, Loki stopped advancing. He took a few steps backward, swayed from one side to the other, and then sat down in the snow.

Erling dismounted from the mule and led him over to a nearby tree. After he tied Loki's reins to a low branch, he continued through the forest on foot. He soon came across two pairs of windswept tracks cutting a jagged route through the snow. They'd been filed down and smoothed over so much that he couldn't tell whether they were coming or going, or if they'd belonged to humans or animals.

He trudged onward, making his way through a stretch of birch trees. Then he fought his way up a steep and icy scarp. After reaching the top of a ridge, he emerged from the forest and saw a scattering of lights at the bottom of a valley. Though he hadn't been there in years, he knew without a doubt that it was the village of Meråker.

Erling descended the hill and approached the village, hoping to find some wire to repair Loki's hoof and perhaps some food as well. He thought about the last time he'd been there, on a trip back from Sweden with Martha. She'd wanted to spend the night for the *Sankthansaften* festivities, but he'd been in a hurry to get back, so they didn't stop. He felt a wave of regret wash over him, wishing he'd acted differently.

He pushed the thoughts from his mind and picked up his pace, wanting to return to Loki before the sunlight had drained away and the curfew was back in effect. He soon emerged from the trees and saw the outskirts of the small village. Before he reached them, though, he spotted a pair of Waffen-SS milling about outside one of the houses. Then he saw a half-track full of more Waffen-SS approaching, and another group of soldiers checking a local's papers by the Meråker Bridge.

Erling stopped and ducked behind a stand of trees. He counted the German soldiers. There were at least fifty that he could see, and he knew that there had to be more inside or hidden from his view. He counted a dozen vehicles as well, including two Panzer III tanks. *What was an entire company of Germans doing in Meråker?* he wondered. It didn't seem right; a dozen or two soldiers, maybe, but not an entire company, and certainly no armored tanks.

He soon spotted a farmer riding a horse-drawn cart. He thought about approaching the farmer and asking about the Germans, but if the Germans stopped him, they'd ask him what he was doing all the way out in Meråker, especially without his cart. He slipped back toward the tree line instead and continued along the edge of the village, staying close to the forest. He eventually left the trees near a group of houses and approached the town's main road. In the distance, he spotted the *Handelsforening*, but he avoided it after seeing a group of Waffen-SS outside.

He continued on through the town, spotting more Nazis at the train station, and more outside the town hall as well. After reaching the town center, he turned around and headed back in the direction he'd come from, his thoughts drifting back toward Kari. She must have approached Meråker on her way east, he assumed. With all the Nazis there, though, she couldn't have passed through it with the Allied pilot. He wondered what she'd done, then wondered about the remainder of her route heading east. If the Germans were protecting Meråker, they must be protecting Kopperå and all the other villages from there to Sweden, as well as all of the stations, mills, and dams. Kari must've have left the trails and headed for the highlands to get to Sweden, he realized. Unless she was no longer heading east, he couldn't think of any other route she would take.

Erling snuck his way toward a barn behind a house

that appeared empty. He opened the barn door and went in, then quietly closed the door behind him. He lit a match and made his way through the dark space. The temperature inside the barn was even lower than it was outside, and it smelled like cat urine and mold. It also seemed to have been deserted for some time; no animals dwelled there, and thick cobwebs hung from the rafters and inside the stalls.

He wandered his way past some rusty farm equipment and approached a cluttered workbench. Then he went through its drawers and shelves, looking for baling wire. He didn't find any, but he found some screws he could use to stabilize the crack in Loki's hoof. He also found a rasp he could use to file down the hoof wall.

Erling put the rasp and screws in his pockets and made his way back toward the barn door. Before he could open it, he heard a commotion outside. He looked through a gap in the wall and saw a group of armed Waffen-SS, walking across the yard. Then he noticed his tracks in the snow, leading directly toward the barn door.

Erling's heart caught in his throat. *Were they looking for him?* he wondered. *Had they found Loki?* He glanced around for a weapon. Other than a rusty pitchfork and a claw hammer, there wasn't anything of use.

He went over to the workbench and grabbed the claw hammer, then crept back toward the barn door. He heard something behind him in the shadows, scratching its way toward him across the dirt floor. He gripped the hammer and raised it, ready to strike. Then he saw two milky eyes emerge from the darkness, sunken at the back of an old dog's face.

The dog began to growl, though it was clear from his skewed glance and cloudy eyes that he couldn't see. Erling reached into his pocket and took out his last strip of jerky. Though his stomach rumbled, he was less afraid of starving than he was of facing a company of Germans. He tossed the jerky across the barn, and the dog ambled after it, disappearing back into the darkness. Erling then turned his attention back toward the Germans. He watched as more soldiers approached, joining the others. Then he looked down at his footprints in the snow. In the fading light, they were still visible.

Erling's heart hammered in his chest. One of the soldiers saw the slightly open barn door and approached it. Erling hid against the wall of the barn and waited, raising the claw hammer again with a trembling hand. The soldier opened the door and entered the barn, and Erling held his breath and waited as the soldier nosed around. He came close to Erling, and for a moment, Erling thought he might have seen him, but then the soldier made his way back to the door and left the barn, sliding the door shut behind him.

Erling turned and peered once more through the gap in the wall, breathing a sigh of relief as he watched the men approach the next house. He waited for a few minutes until he was sure they were gone. Then he put the hammer back on the workbench and left the barn.

He made his way back to the tree line and entered the forest, hurrying his way back toward the foothills where he'd left Loki. His arthritic knee began to throb again, but he grit his teeth and pushed on through the pain. Overhead, a handful of stars burned brightly in the clear night sky.

Erling began to plot his next move. He had to assume that Kari had taken the highlands; she wouldn't have continued following the towns and train lines, with all the Germans in the way. Even if she hadn't headed into the highlands, by taking them, Erling might be able to reach Sweden before her and start backtracking from there. If she'd gone south or west for any reason, there wasn't anything he could do, and he wasn't ready to consider the possibility that she'd gotten caught, either.

He made up his mind. After he finished repairing the crack in Loki's hoof, he'd dig up whatever grass he could find and feed and water the mule. Then he'd set out toward the highlands, riding all night. If Loki's hoof held out, he should be able to get to Sweden by the following afternoon. Even if it didn't and he had to continue on foot, he could probably make it by the evening.

He approached the last hill leading toward the spot where he'd left Loki. He bounded his way up the hill, hardly noticing his throbbing knee. He decided that when he found Kari, he wouldn't be angry. Instead, he'd express his relief, grateful that she was safe.

Before he could reach the crest of the hill, Erling heard a brief, hollow sound in the distance, like a popping champagne cork. Then a sharp, scratching noise followed it. He stopped in his tracks, then watched as a flare exploded in the sky, releasing a bright red starburst that pierced the night. He watched the brilliant light for a moment as it slowly descended toward the ground, oddly beautiful and out of place. Then he snapped out of his reverie, realizing with horror that the flare had been fired from where he'd left the mule.

He hurried his way toward the origin of the flare, going from one tree to the next and staying in the shadows. His heart pounded in his chest, and he felt dizzy and sick. He approached the clearing where he'd left Loki, and through the trees, he spotted a Norwegian farmer standing next to the mule. Then he saw a pair of armed Waffen-SS talking to the farmer.

One of them was holding Erling's rifle.

CHAPTER 16

Kari and Lance rode through the night, climbing steadily into the highlands. The air grew colder and thinner the further they went, and Torden's breathing grew increasingly labored. At one point, they encountered the trail of a fox, zigzagging its way across the landscape. They followed the trail for a while, until it turned sharply and switchbacked toward the lower valley. Then they continued onward, forging their way across the unmarked snow.

The snowfall picked up, though it was hardly discernible in the darkness. Kari could feel it, though, the way the bigger flakes brushed against her skin and lingered on her clothing. She could hear it as well, dampening Torden's footfalls and the sound of his ragged breathing. She urged Torden onward, and they clambered up over an icy ridge and down toward a barren dale.

Torden slipped along the decline, balking and nickering until he rediscovered his footing. Then he picked his way forward, one deliberate step at a time. After Torden slipped again, he pulled up and whinnied, refusing to proceed further until Kari dug her heels into his sides. She scanned the horizon, looking for cover. The clouds were low and the night was tar black, and it was impossible to see in the thickening snow; even the mountains in the background had disappeared, retreating into the void. The world before them was an apparition, as murky and shifting as a river after a storm.

Lance spoke.

"We should stop," he said.

"We need to find cover," said Kari.

She kicked Torden's flanks, and they continued on into the valley. The temperature dropped further, and the winds picked up with nothing to impede them, blinding them with icy dust and penetrating every gap and stitch in their clothing. Torden stumbled again, and they nearly fell off as he struggled to stay afoot. Lance grabbed Kari by the shoulder and spoke loudly over the lashing wind.

"We really should stop," he said.

Ignoring him, she continued to look toward the horizon, finally spotting a stand of pine trees about a kilometer away.

"Over there," she said, urging the horse onward.

It took them almost half an hour to cover a distance that should've taken minutes. The biting wind forced water from the corners of their eyes and rattled their teeth, and by the time they finally reached the trees, Kari could hardly feel her fingers or toes. They dismounted from the horse and looked for shelter. Kari spotted a gap between a few thick spruce trees where little snow had reached the ground. She led Torden toward it and tied him to one of its lower branches. Then she and Lance began to gather wood.

Once they had enough, Kari cleared away a section of the forest floor. After she got through the snow, she tried to dig into the frozen earth, but her numb fingers refused to work. Lance took over, using a stick to get a hole started and then a flat rock to dig deeper into the hard ground. After he dug a pit about a meter wide and a half a meter deep, they went to look for kindling.

They gathered the few dry sticks and leaves they could find until they had a pile the size of a hawk's nest. Then Lance used his knife to shave some bark onto the small mound. He took out his Zippo and struggled to ignite it, but his fingers had also gone numb. He wrung out his hands and tried again, eventually managing to ignite the wick.

He lit the pile of tinder, bending over it to shield it from the menacing wind. The fire took hold in the bark scrapings, then spread to the leaves and sticks. Once they were burning, Lance stacked a few frozen logs onto the pile. At first, they didn't catch, but after the fire melted the frost on them, the logs slowly began to burn.

Kari and Lance ventured out to gather more wood. Once they'd collected enough to last the night, they approached the fire and huddled over it, extending their hands to the flames. They alternated warming their front and backsides until they weren't shivering anymore. Before long, Kari was able to open and close her fingers again, and not long after that, she could feel her toes as well.

The winds fell and rose and then fell again, and the clouds shifted and broke, opening a vast window to the heavens. The stars emerged bright and clear in the inky night, glittering like bits of mica in a stone. The God's Nail shined directly overhead, in the center of the sky; Thjazi's Eyes gleamed in the southeast, where Odin had cast them after battle, and Loki's Torch burned to the south above Oslo, brighter than them all.

They warmed themselves by the fire, hanging their wet coats on the low branches to dry them. They sat there until the winds died down and the logs dwindled to husks of ash, then piled more wood onto the blaze and waited for the flames to take hold. After a while, Kari's stomach rumbled. Embarrassed, she looked away from Lance, but a moment later, her stomach whined again. Lance rose.

"I'll look for some food—"

She stood before he could finish.

"I'll go," she said.

"You sure?"

She nodded.

"I know this area," she said, pulling on her coat. Before he could reply, she took the pistol and headed off into the darkness, making her way through the forest and heading toward a nearby valley. The area was full of deer, elk, and rabbit, and it was home to bears and wolves as well. She'd hunted the hills as a girl, pegging squirrels and ptarmigans with a single-shot .22-caliber *guttekarabin*. Most of the animals were asleep now, but there were still some night feeders out, judging by the fresh tracks in the snow.

After a while, the snow stopped falling and the winds died down, but it remained biting cold. Before Kari had gotten far from their makeshift camp, the warmth from the fire had vanished from her clothing. She raised her collar and pulled down her hat, then shoved her fists into her pockets and continued on her way. She soon found the trail of a young hare, its oval-shaped tracks barely puncturing the icy crust of the snow.

Kari followed the trail as it wound past a copse of trees and through a patch of barren cloudberry bushes. Halfway across an open field, the tracks abruptly ended. Most likely, the animal had been snatched there by a hawk or some other bird of prey.

She continued on, and after she crossed the open field, she made her way up a rocky incline. Once she reached its peak, she looked over her shoulder, toward their makeshift camp. The fire looked so small and so far away, though it couldn't have been more than a kilometer from her. She wondered what Lance was doing, and if he was thinking of her, then pushed the thought from her mind and trudged onward.

She followed the ridgeline for a while and then made her way down toward a wooded vale, crossing a field full of waist-high bushes that would soon begin to bloom. Approaching the trees, she heard the soft, low-pitched hooting of a grey owl in the distance. Where there were owls, she assumed, there were likely weasels and other small game. Exhausted and famished, she would've settled for a squirrel at that point, or even a rat.

Kari wandered through a maze of naked birch trees and shrubs, and she soon picked up another set of tracks. They were different from the hare's, deeper and more spaced-out, like those of a fox. She slowed her pace as she continued on, picking her way across the rocks and ice so she wouldn't spook her prey. Then she made her way down another decline, following the animal's zigzagging path. The tracks grew fresher the further she went, and she soon spotted movement in the distance, by some bushes near the base of the hill.

She stalked her quarry, and before long, she saw something short and fat waddling through the underbrush. At first, she thought it might be a wood grouse or a hedgehog. When she crept closer, though, she realized it was a badger. She followed the animal for some time, pausing when it stopped and resuming pursuit when it continued. She kept as quiet as she could, moving slowly and letting the snow muffle her footfalls. Kari drew the pistol when she could see the white stripes along the badger's back, then raised the pistol and took aim. *Square your stance*, she could hear her grandfather say. *Align your sights. Take a breath and let it out naturally until it stops on its own. Then press the trigger.*

After a moment, she fired, and the pistol jumped in her hand as it discharged. Though muffled by the snowfall, the gunshot exploded through the forest and rang in her ears. The badger flopped forward into the snow, stretched out wide and as motionless as a rug. A fine mist of blood fanned out in the snow before it in a bright red spray.

Kari lowered the pistol and approached the fallen animal. She looked down when she reached it, seeing a coin-sized hole in the center of its back. She picked it up by its hind legs and it flopped over, revealing a bloody cavity where the slug had exited its body. There didn't seem to be much meat on it, but it seemed more substantial than Lance's D-ration bars, and it probably tasted better, too.

She carried the animal back in the direction of the camp, following her own wandering tracks. While making her way up the ridgeline, she imagined Lance greeting her upon her return. She envisioned him grinning, shaking his head in a mixture of pride and disbelief. Barely able to contain her excitement, she had to keep herself from breaking into a run.

Kari hesitated as she approached a frozen creek. She put down the badger, then looked at her image in the ice. Even though it was dark and the ice was blurry, she could make out her reflection, and she felt embarrassed for looking so plain. She slapped her cheeks until there was some color in them, then took off her hat and mussed her hair, trying to fashion it like Rita Hayworth's. After a moment, she looked at her reflection again; she didn't look anything like Hayworth, but she looked better than she had, and as good as she would given the circumstances.

She picked up the badger and continued on her way, soon approaching the stand of trees where they'd made their camp. She spotted the fire first, its flames dancing in the wind. Then she saw Lance's coat hanging from a branch near the fire, and the shape of Torden in the shadows. Lance, however, was nowhere to be seen.

Kari dropped the badger and ran toward the fire, her heartbeat quickening. She entered the clearing and saw Lance, lying on his side with his back to her. Her first thought was that he'd been shot by a sniper or stabbed in the gut.

After she approached him and knelt down, though, she heard his snoring, realizing with a mixture of disappointment and relief that he'd only fallen asleep.

CHAPTER 17

The first faint smudges of dawn began to emerge on the horizon. At the onset, they were barely perceptible, little more than smears on a lampblack canvas. Then they swelled into patches, and then shapes. Before long, they fused into a mottled grey tapestry, forcing the fading moon to retreat into the background.

Moltke and his men rode the remaining half-track along a winding country trail, following the soldier on the motorcycle. Though he'd hardly slept in days, Moltke was alert and excited at the prospect of finishing the assignment and returning to Trondheim. In his mind, he'd composed a draft of the letter he'd send to the Brigade General, coming up with a way to sound determined yet still respectful. He'd also begun toying with the idea of asking a friend in the Gestapo to help him locate Elise. If he was going to take some risks, he figured, why not consider taking that one as well?

They continued their zigzagging advance through the forest, going slowly enough to prevent from sliding around corners or slipping on the ice patches that had formed overnight. Moltke looked for ways to distract himself, as he grew increasingly impatient along the way. He counted the passing birch trees first, reaching a hundred, and then two hundred, only growing even more anxious from the mindless repetition. Then he began to hum Mozart's 40th Symphony, as the sound of the groaning engine reminded him of its aggressive tempo.

After a while, a few sets of tire tracks appeared in the snow, made by what looked like Opel Blitzes or heavy, off-road Einheits-PKW. They continued on, picking up their speed as they drove in the tracks. Before long, they rounded a bend in the road and descended into a valley. After going around another curve, they approached another motorcycle and a pair of six-wheeled Krupp Protzes, parked off to the side of the road. A dozen soldiers milled about, smoking unfiltered Ecksteins and blowing onto their bare hands.

Schweitzer pulled over and parked the half-track, and Moltke and his men got out and approached the others. Moltke looked around for the commanding officer, and when an older soldier with the flattened face of a pugilist stepped forward, Moltke addressed him before the man could even finish his salute.

"Where's the body?" said Moltke.

"Over there," said the soldier, pointing toward another group of soldiers standing by a frozen creek.

Moltke and his men made their way down a twisting path and approached the creek. The soldiers parted as Moltke's men came near, revealing the body of an Allied airman lying facedown in the shallows. Goetz and Schweitzer knelt down and struggled to turn over the stiffened corpse, which had frozen to the earth. It sounded like paper tearing when they finally managed to pull it free, and they rolled it over, revealing the airman's frostbitten face.

Moltke knelt down and examined the body. The airman's leather jacket was as stiff as cardboard, and his vacant eyes gazed blankly toward the horizon. His pupils had an odd, blue-white haze to them, and the eyeballs themselves looked soft and flattened, like old grapes. His right arm had frozen in a raised and extended position, as if he was trying to get something that was just out of reach. Pale and frozen, it reminded Moltke of the Greek statues he'd seen as a boy at the Altes Museum in Berlin.

"It looks like our man," said Goetz, pointing to the flight patches on the man's jacket.

Moltke hesitated. *It was the body of a U.S. airman, but was it the same airman from the plane they'd found?* he wondered. He seemed to be a long way from the crash site, and he seemed to have been dead for some time, judging by his waxy, grayish-yellow skin. There was no nametag or dog tags, though, so it was impossible to confirm.

"What do you want to do, sir?" asked Schweitzer.

Moltke continued to look over the body, unsure. He envisioned himself wandering the frozen wasteland for weeks, searching for a corpse that might remain buried until summer. Then he visualized being back in Trondheim, packing his things and preparing to go to Africa. He saw himself leading an armored tank division through Cyrenaica alongside Rommel, then imagined celebrating with Elise at the Hotel Majestic in Tunis.

After a moment, Moltke stood.

"Send the body to Falstad," he said, walking in the direction of the half-track. "We're finished here."

A wolf howled past the dawn, its lonely wail carrying down from the mountains. For a while, it was the only sound in the valley, sobbing in the darkness like someone recently bereaved. Before long, it was joined by birdsong and other harbingers of the approaching day. It eventually faded into the background before finally disappearing, replaced by a growing chorus of grosbeaks and redpolls.

Sverre pedaled his bicycle toward Hegra, humming along with the birds. He hadn't slept, and he hadn't eaten, either, but he felt energetic and alive, and much better than he'd felt in years. He'd spent the entire night planning what he was going to do once Moltke returned the family farm to him for helping them find the pilot. He needed to get a herd first; that was the most important thing. *After all*, he figured, *what's a dairy farm without any cows?* Without the money, it would be difficult, but he could surely get a loan, having the farm as collateral. Once that was taken care of, it was on to planting; it was too late for potatoes, but he might be able to get the barley in on time. He also wanted to repaint the house its original red, covering the garish yellow those idiot Southerners had painted it when they'd taken it over.

Rounding a bend in the road, Sverre was so deep in thought that he nearly crashed into a horse pulling a cart full of lumber. The driver of the cart yanked up on the reins to avoid hitting him, and the horse lurched off the narrow road, causing the contents of the cart to tumble to the ground. The driver cursed and shook his fist at Sverre.

"Sorry," said Sverre, riding past without stopping.

He continued on and soon pedaled into town, then turned onto the main street, passing the grocery store and then the *rådhus*. After turning at the train station, he approached the hotel that the SS had taken over. He hopped off the bicycle before it had come to a stop and leaned it against a tree. Then he composed himself before going inside.

A flood of memories washed over Sverre as he went into the hotel. It was just as he'd remembered from the last time he'd been there, as a boy, for an Easter supper with his family; the dark wood paneling on the walls gleamed in the firelight, and the dour subjects of the paintings remained as they'd been, unaltered by the passing of time. Everything was exactly the same—except for the Nazi flags that had replaced the Norwegian ones, and the Waffen-SS milling about.

An officious-looking desk clerk addressed Sverre when he saw him, unable to hide his disdain for Sverre's appearance.

"May I help you?" he said, speaking in German.

Sverre replied in Norwegian.

"I'm here to see the Oberleutnant," he said.

"And what's this in regard to?"

"It's official business."

The desk clerk narrowed his gaze.

"Call him," said Sverre. "You'll see."

The desk clerk picked up a telephone and pointed to some chairs by a fireplace.

"Have a seat," he said.

"That's all right," said Sverre. "I'll stand."

The desk clerk turned his back to Sverre and dialed one of the rooms. Sverre felt his hands instinctively ball into fists, but he held himself back from going after the desk clerk, knowing that it wasn't the right time. He envisioned himself returning to the hotel later that year, wearing a new suit and with a beautiful woman on his arm. He imagined himself checking into the hotel's best room, then ordering the desk clerk around day and night. Then he took it a step further, seeing himself buying the hotel and firing the desk clerk, kicking him out into the street. The intoxicating feeling of vengeance quickly replaced his simmering resentment.

After the desk clerk had a brief conversation in German with the person at the other end of the line, he hung up and turned back to Sverre.

"The Oberleutnant won't see you," he said.

The new suit and the beautiful woman evaporated from Sverre's fantasy, replaced by his threadbare clothes and the toady desk clerk.

"I beg your pardon?" said Sverre.

"I'm sorry—"

Sverre interrupted the desk clerk.

"There must be a mistake," he said, making his way back toward the stairwell.

"Sir, you can't go up there—"

Sverre pushed his way past the desk clerk, and the desk clerk called after him.

"Sir!"

Sverre ignored the desk clerk, but before he got far, the desk clerk motioned to a pair of Waffen-SS, who went after Sverre.

"Come on," said one of the soldiers, grabbing Sverre's arm.

"Let go of me—"

The soldiers dragged Sverre toward the hotel entrance. Sverre shouted up toward the rooms.

"Herr Oberleutnant!"

Ignoring him, the soldiers forced Sverre outside,

where they shoved him into a snowdrift.

"Stay out," said one of the soldiers.

Sverre scrambled to his feet, his hands again balling into fists.

"You bastards—"

"Are you deaf?" said the other soldier, knocking him back to the ground. "Get out of here, or you're a dead man."

Sverre glared at the soldier, his cheeks burning with rage. He looked around at the gathering crowd, then looked back to the soldier, who stood firm. The other soldier stood next to him, his hand on the holster of his pistol.

After a long moment, Sverre got up and approached his bicycle. Then he climbed onto it and pedaled away.

CHAPTER 18

Kari dreamed that it was summer, and that she was wandering toward the highlands past their farm. She was looking for cloudberries, as she and her mother often did during long July evenings, when the sun would stay out until midnight. They'd fill baskets and bring them back home, serving them with fresh cream or baking them into pies and crumbles. Whatever they didn't eat, they'd turn into preserves for the endless winters ahead.

She trudged her way up a wooded hill and entered a meadow. The area was an explosion of color, carpeted with orange hawkweed, Nordic ginseng, and woodland cranesbill. Overhead, the sun shined so brightly that it caused her to squint. She closed her eyes and continued on, breathing in deep lungsful of the perfumed air.

After crossing the meadow, she reentered the forest, climbing further into the mountains under a thick canopy of evergreens. The forest was darker and cooler than the open meadow, and it was quieter, too. It felt like it was hiding something. Secrets, perhaps; the black earth underfoot was full of treasure, and full of bones.

A hawk took flight from a high perch, soundless in its exit, and somewhere in the distance, water ran through the wilderness. Kari made her way up a low ridge and then out into another meadow full of scrub and ragged brush. She soon saw her first cloudberry bush, its tiny, golden fruit dangling at the end of its stalk. Then she saw another, and another. Before long, she found an entire galaxy of them.

She bent down and began to gather the ripe berries. Some of the drupelets burst when she plucked the fruit off the stalks, staining her fingertips with a golden syrup. She kept dropping them into her basket, one after the other, but no matter how many she picked, the basket remained empty. She increased her pace, but the basket still wouldn't fill, and the berries in front of her proliferated, multiplying like splitting cells.

She fought the urge to panic, finding it difficult to breathe. The sound of running water grew in the forest all around her, slowly building from a whisper to a roar. Curious, she stopped picking berries and began to look for the water's source, soon finding a river. She approached the riverbank and knelt down to look at her reflection.

Instead of seeing her own face staring back at her, though, she saw the face of her father, his empty eyes clouded over.

The wind came down from the mountain and shook the branches, loosing snow from sagging limbs and rattling the forest. It curled around the tree trunks and ran down the valleys and coursed over stone. Wherever it met resistance, it found other pathways to advance. Then, as quickly as it had arrived, it disappeared again, moving off toward the west.

After feeling the wind wash over her, Kari opened her eyes. She saw the tree branches above her, crusted with ice. Then she saw the concrete sky, smudged with thick cirrocumulus. She glanced over and saw the empty space next to her, where Lance had been sleeping. Turning around, she spotted him across the fire, squatting on his haunches and smoking a cigarette.

"You all right?" he asked.

She nodded. He took one last drag off the cigarette, then flicked the butt toward the fire and stood up.

"We better get going," he said.

A herd of goats boiled up a steep ridge, browsing for food. They spread out, clambering across the icy rocks and nibbling on whatever shrubs and weeds they could find.

An older buck tried to edge a kid away from the frozen shoots it was eating, but the kid made a run at the buck and head-butted him in the ribs. A goat herder followed them from a distance, sucking an unlit briar pipe and leaving the animals to sort out their differences themselves.

Sverre pedaled his bicycle along the dirt road leading to the Dahlstrøm farmhouse, fighting his way through the snow. Though he tried not to think about it, he kept reliving the scene back in Hegra. Instead of a few people gathering to watch, though, he saw a dozen, and then a few dozen, and then the entire town. They kept coming and coming until it seemed like the whole county was there, and the chorus of their laughter swelled and built toward a crescendo.

He screamed out loud, trying to purge the hideous sound from his mind. His cry shattered the silence of the forest, and a bird took flight from a branch and flapped off into the distance. For a moment, he worried about what people might think if they saw him screaming as he rode his bicycle through an empty forest. *Am I going crazy?* he wondered. *Did I see what I thought I saw, or did I just imagine it?* Then he quickly shook the thought from his mind, refusing to consider it. *No*, he thought, *I know what I saw, and I know that Erling's up to something. To hell with what people think, anyway.*

He fought his way up the hill, fueled by rage, not needing to stop this time and push the bicycle on foot.

Then he continued past the Prestrud's property, unwilling to take the extra time to go around it. When he approached the Dahlstrøm farm, he jumped off his bicycle without even bothering to come to a stop, letting it fall clunking to the snow. Then he went forward and searched the area.

He made his way toward the barn, where a number of recent tracks marked the snow. Too wide and too deep to be cart tracks, he assumed they'd been made by the Germans' vehicles. He pushed open the barn door and went inside. This time, the sheep hardly paid him any attention; they'd clearly been watered and fed since he was there, and some bits of silage still lay in their trough.

Unsettled, Sverre left the barn. *Am I going crazy?* he wondered again. It took longer to shake the thoughts from his mind, as they gained strength while his certainty diminished. He recalled a line from a play he'd read as a young man, still fresh after decades of dormancy. *"Oh, full of scorpions is my mind, dear wife..."* Maybe I am going crazy, he thought again. Then another voice spoke in his mind, a louder voice that reminded Sverre of his father. *Shut up*, it said. *You're not crazy. You know exactly what you saw... now go out and prove it.*

Emboldened, Sverre made his way across the property and approached the farmhouse. No smoke rose from its chimney, and no lanterns or candles burned inside. He looked inside each of the windows, but he didn't see anyone; the farmhouse appeared empty. He approached the kitchen window, then looked around to see if anyone was watching him. There was no one there, though the forest seemed to contain thousands of eyes.

Sverre turned back to the kitchen window, then smashed it with his elbow. He reached in through the broken glass and unfastened the latch, then raised the window and climbed inside. He wandered through the kitchen, making his way to the stove. Then he opened its grate and looked inside; he stirred the ashes with a finger, and they were cold, scattering from his touch.

Sverre approached the sink and looked into it, seeing a bowl. He picked it up and ran his index finger across it, noticing that it was still moist. *Someone must've been there that morning,* he assumed. *But how could that be,* he wondered, *and where were they now?* He put down the bowl and continued through the house, going from room to room, looking for clues. If they did leave, they left in a hurry, and they didn't take anything or leave anything behind that shed light on their whereabouts or plans.

Sverre finally left the house, dejected. He wandered the property looking for tracks or other indications of what Erling and his daughter were doing, or where they had gone. The only footprints he saw other than the Germans', though, were his own.

He started to wonder again if he'd been mistaken, then began to worry once more that he was losing his mind. Before he got back to his bicycle, he noticed a set of tracks leading back behind the barn. They weren't new tracks, like the others; they'd been filed down by the winds and obscured by the snowfall. There might even have been two sets of tracks, for all he could tell; they looked more like mountain ranges than footprints, yet there they were, clearly advancing toward the barn. It made sense that he didn't see them his first time through, as they were somewhat concealed, but now that he did see them, they were impossible to miss.

Sverre followed the tracks, gaining speed as if he were travelling downhill. He broke into a trot, stumbling onward through the snow. The tracks came to an end behind the barn near what looked like the outline of a fire pit. He knelt down and cleared away the snow, using his bare hands to dig.

Among the ashes at the bottom of the fire pit, he found a burnt scrap of an Allied squadron patch.

CHAPTER 19

A lynx descended into the lowlands, stalking the trail of a roe deer into the taiga. The deer's tracks were three times the size of the lynx's, but prey was scarce, and the lynx was famished. It avoided the steppe and the deeper snows, keeping to the spruce and birch that filled the lower valley. Its thick, greyish-brown coat blended seamlessly with its surroundings, and it moved soundlessly across the harsh landscape.

The lynx left the trail of the deer and cut across a stretch of woodlands, hoping to ambush its prey. After finishing a semi-circle through the forest, it doubled back and prepared to strike. Before it got the chance, it heard something break through the ice crust nearby. Hearing more crunching ice, it slipped off into the wilderness, preferring to leave its quarry than to face an unknown threat.

After a moment, a camouflaged soldier emerged from the snow-swept tree line, cradling a bolt-action rifle. Then another soldier emerged from the forest, and another. Before long, an entire *Gebirgsjäger* unit appeared, the distinctive *Edelweiß* insignias on their caps and sleeves. Armed with light machine guns and dressed all in white, they passed as quietly as clouds across the sky.

They moved forward through the forest, searching the area. Earlier that day, they'd received intelligence that the Norwegian Resistance was escorting an OSS unit from Sweden. Embarrassed by the sabotage at Vemork and the Inter-Allied Commando raids in Lofoten and Måløy, the Reichskommissar had sent a number of *Gebirgsjäger* units to patrol the area. He'd wanted to act swiftly and brutally, quelling the possibility of further defiance.

Before long, one of the soldiers spotted some wandering tracks in the distance. He peeled off from the unit to get a better look at them. Smoothed over by the wind and covered by the recent snow, it was impossible to tell whether a person or an animal had made them. Not wanting to take a chance, he continued to follow them as they wound deeper into the forest.

The soldier soon entered a clearing and found an abandoned campfire. The area around the fire was littered with footprints, the treads of the soles still visible in many of them. The soldier went forward and knelt down next to the footprints, examining them. He noticed they had the distinctive impressions made by the slanted heels of jump boots.

He also spotted a cigarette butt near the fire, the 'LUCKY STRIKE' logo clearly printed on its side.

The wind rose up and passed through Hegra, knocking the snow loose from the branches and shaking the windows. A group of people stood in line outside the *Handelsforening*, waiting for their food rations. After a moment, a pregnant woman wearing a *Lebensborn* pin on her coat exited the store, carrying a large bag of groceries. Some of the people in line spat at the ground behind her, muttering things like 'traitor' or 'Nazi whore' as she walked past.

Sverre rode into town, pedaling as fast as he could but keeping the bicycle under control. He focused on the task, suppressing the urge to get ahead of himself again. There would be plenty of time for planning later, once the farm was back in his possession. For now, though, his only goal was to prove to Moltke that he'd been right.

He slowed the bicycle as he approached the hotel. Then he hopped off it and leaned it against a tree, near a parked police motorcycle. He went inside and walked past the desk clerk without acknowledging him.

"Sir—"

Before the desk clerk could finish, Sverre was already halfway up the stairs. The desk clerk hurried up the stairs after him.

"Sir!"

Ignoring the desk clerk, Sverre pounded on each room's door.

"Herr Oberleutnant?"

The desk clerk tried to stop him.

"You can't do that—"

Continuing to ignore him, Sverre pounded on the next door.

"Herr Oberleutnant!"

The desk clerk tried to stop Sverre again.

"He's not here—"

Sverre spun around and shoved the desk clerk against the wall.

"Where is he?" he said.

"I don't know—"

Sverre pulled out a rusty pocketknife and put the blade to the desk clerk's throat.

"You lie," he said, spitting the words through his *snus*-stained teeth.

"He got a call this morning, about the downed pilot," said the desk clerk. "He and his men left in a hurry."

"Where?"

"I don't know—"

Sverre jabbed the point of the blade into the desk clerk's neck, drawing blood.

"I swear, I don't know," said the desk clerk, closing his eyes.

Sverre hesitated.

"Please," said the desk clerk. "Don't kill me."

After a long moment, Sverre lowered the pocketknife and released the desk clerk. Then he hurried back down the stairs as the desk clerk slid whimpering to the floor, clutching his throat.

CHAPTER 20

The Stjørdal River began near the Norwegian-Swedish border, at the confluence of the Dalåa and the Torsbjørka. It wound its way westward from there, gaining momentum as the Kåpperåa, the Funna, and the Forra fed into it. By the time it reached the stony highlands of Nord-Trøndelag, it churned fast and white, often swelling as wide as a soccer pitch. Its music rose and ebbed along the way, changing back and forth from a murmur to a roar.

Erling trudged his way up through the highlands, going east in the direction he assumed Kari was heading and following the Stjørdal back toward its source. He travelled through the night and into midday without a break, knowing she'd be going twice as fast as him on horseback, if not faster. He'd jog until he grew winded, gritting his teeth and fighting through the pain of his arthritic knee. Then he'd walk for a spell until he got his breath back, and then he'd jog some more until he was gasping again.

By the time the sun reached its apex, Erling's clothes were soaked with sweat, even though the temperature hovered around the freezing point. The bottoms of his feet were mottled with blisters, and he slipped and slid in his blood and pus-soaked socks. He hadn't eaten all day, and his throat was a desert. He scooped up a big handful of snow and ate it without stopping, then struggled his way up a treacherous ridge.

After reaching the crest, Erling began to descend toward a narrow valley. He saw something glinting in the distance to the south, reflecting the wan sunlight. Afraid it was the glass of a riflescope or an enemy's windshield, he took cover in the wilderness. After continuing through the forest for a few hundred meters, though, he realized it was only a cabin window.

Erling slowed his pace and considered his options. He could see if there was anything of use in the cabin; if he was lucky, there might be some skis, or at least a rifle or something to eat. If he stopped, though, every second he spent there was a second that Kari was getting further away from him. But if he continued at his current pace, she was still pulling away, just at a slightly slower rate; he'd never catch her, unless she stopped or turned back.

After a moment of deliberation, Erling changed

directions and headed south toward the cabin. He broke into a trot, wanting to spend as little time as possible on the detour. He soon approached the small cabin, noticing the snowdrift covering its door. The cap of its stove chimney was buried in snow as well; it looked like no one had been there in months, if not years.

Erling peered in through one of the cabin's windows, but he saw nothing inside, other than a set of antlers on one wall. He cleared away the snow from the door and tried the handle, but it wouldn't budge. Remembering the rasp in his coat pocket, he took it out and forced it between the door and the doorframe. Then he pried open the door.

He stepped inside the cabin. It smelled faintly of pinesap and mushrooms, and in the closed space of the cabin, he suddenly became aware of his own stench. There was just enough light to see the cabin's meager furnishings—a table and a chair, a small bed, and a rusty stove. A few books sat on a shelf, including a worn botanical atlas and a copy of Fridtjof Nansen's *Fram over Polhavet*. To Erling's surprise and relief, he also spotted a pair of old wooden skis propped against the wall.

Erling approached the skis and inspected them. They were short, probably belonging to a woman or a child, and the thong bindings were coming apart, but they'd be a vast improvement over walking. He searched the cabin for poles, but there weren't any to be found. *No matter*, he figured; he could use sticks instead.

He looked through the rest of the cabin, searching for weapons or food. He found a rusty, bolt-action hunting rifle, but there were no cartridges. He searched the cabin again—still no luck—but he found an old wooden bow underneath the bed, along with a few target arrows. He picked up the bow and pulled back on the bowstring, testing the draw. It was a bit slack, but it was better than nothing.

He found a few tins of King Oscar sardines in a cupboard and shoved them into his pocket. Then he slung the bow over his shoulder and exited the cabin. Outside, he looked for branches that could pass as poles. After finding a pair, he placed the skis on the snow. Then he stepped into the bindings and pulled them tight. One of them was already coming apart, so he cut a strip from his undershirt and used it to tie the binding to the ski. Then he dug into the snow with the makeshift poles and set out back in the direction he'd been heading.

The skis were small, and the bindings were loose, but Erling travelled much faster on the skis than he did on foot. He was rusty at the start—he was never much of a skier in the first place—but he soon got the hang of it, pushing further with each stride. Once he settled into a rhythm, he took out a tin of sardines and opened it, scooping some into his mouth. They tasted like battery acid, metallic and sour. He spat them out and tossed aside the tin, then opened another—they'd also gone bad. So had the third tin. He threw them aside and continued on, his stomach rumbling.

He fought up a steep incline, then coasted down into a valley. He soon saw a pine tree in the distance, its snow-laden boughs sagging back toward the earth. For some reason, it made him think of Martha, and the way she used to brush her hair before going to bed. He reminisced about a trip he'd taken with her to Sweden, when she was five months pregnant with Kari. He'd told her that she should have stayed home, but she wouldn't listen. She never did; she was so stubborn and independent, qualities that had made their relationship challenging though they were the qualities that had drawn him to her in the first place. At one point during the journey, she'd wanted to discuss baby names. They'd both been against naming the baby after his grandfather if it was a boy, which had been the custom of the time. She'd liked the name Jens, the name of her late uncle. If it was a girl, she also didn't want to give the child a family name, finding Gudrun, Aslaug, and Hjørdis all so dour and old-fashioned. She was going to be her own person, Martha argued, and she should have her own name. Something strong and beautiful, like Ylva, which meant wolf, or Kari, the name for the god of wind.

Before long, Erling heard a humming noise in the distance. It was tinny and scraping at first, like the sound of a revving chainsaw. Then it deepened in pitch and grew louder as it approached, soon rumbling like thunder. He looked toward the sky and spotted a German bomber on the horizon, heading in his direction. He hurried over to some trees, taking cover beneath the branches. Then he waited for the bomber to pass. He looked up as it approached and saw the thick black *Balkenkreuze* on the undersurfaces of its wings.

Once the plane was gone, he emerged from where he'd been hiding and continued toward the border, picking up his pace.

CHAPTER 21

The half-track rumbled through the highlands, following ghost tracks in the snow. It churned its way up rocky hills and barreled across rut-filled meadows. The men smashed their tailbones against their seats whenever the vehicle crashed down, and they piled up into each other on every turn. Even if they'd wanted to speak, it would've been impossible to hear over the groaning engine.

Moltke sat next to Schweitzer in the front of the half-track, staring out at the snow-swept wilderness before them. He was no longer comfortable sitting passively in back, overseeing things from a distance. If the pilot had reached Sweden, he'd be the one who'd answer for it, and his transfer papers would never come through. In fact, he'd probably end up at Falstad, digging ditches, or worse. Knowing this, he hadn't even bothered to wait for Goetz to finish dressing back at Hegra, leaving him behind.

Schweitzer slowed the half-track going around a bend. Moltke turned to him, incredulous.

"What are you doing?" he shouted. "Speed up!"

Schweitzer increased their speed, but when he slowed down again on the next decline, Moltke erupted, grabbing the wheel.

"Stop the vehicle," he said.

"What—?"

Moltke interrupted him, shouting.

"I said stop the vehicle! Now!"

Schweitzer stopped the half-track, and Moltke reached across Schweitzer's lap and pushed open the door.

"Now get out," he said, shoving Schweitzer to the snow.

Before Schweitzer could get back to his feet, Moltke climbed behind the wheel and threw the half-track into gear, pulling away. After a moment, he turned to the two wide-eyed men sitting in back.

"Anyone else want to walk?" he said.

The men shook their heads. Moltke turned around and looked forward again, grinding the gears as he shifted up from second into third.

Somewhere behind the clouds to the west, the sun began to sink toward the horizon, dragging the remaining daylight with it. The winds picked up, knifing their way through the birch and pine. The birds and the rodents disappeared into their nests and burrows, retreating from the advancing darkness. As the temperature dropped, the lake ice cracked and shrank, echoing throughout the silence.

Moltke raced the half-track up a slanting hill, nearly flipping it as he barreled over the hill's crest. Riding down the other side, he noticed a quartet of vehicles in the distance, *Wehrmacht* bar crosses clearly visible on their doors. He soon saw a dozen Waffen-SS, patrolling the area in small groups. Then he saw a number of *Gebirgsjäger* in their all-white uniforms, hardly discernible from their surroundings.

He parked the half-track near the other vehicles and got out, not bothering to see what his remaining men did. Then he made his way toward a grizzled Oberfeldwebel addressing some soldiers and interrupted their conversation.

"Where are the tracks?" he said.

The Oberfeldwebel nodded toward a group of trees, where the remains of a campfire had been cordoned off. Moltke looked at the footprints around the campfire, then looked back to the Oberfeldwebel.

"And what makes you think these belong to an Allied pilot?" he asked.

"They're slanted, like their jump boots."

"Maybe someone found his jump boots."

The Oberfeldwebel held up a cigarette butt.

"Someone find his Lucky Strikes, too?"

Before Moltke could reply, he heard a nasally voice with a singsong Bavarian accent behind him.

"Well, well, if it isn't Clever Hans."

Moltke turned to see Major Aloysius Stahl, the head of the most-decorated company in the Wehrmacht's 20th Mountain Army. Though a wisp of a man, Stahl carried himself like Goliath, and the soldiers gave him a wide berth.

Moltke tried to recover, snapping off a quick salute.

"Heil Hitler—"

Stahl cut him off before he could finish.

"You wasted two days for me," he said. "I should be in Petsamo by now."

"I take full responsibility—"

Stahl cut him off again.

"Of course you take full responsibility, Herr Oberleutnant, and if you don't find that pilot before he leaves the country, you'll never leave this country alive," he said. "Are we understood?"

Before Moltke could reply, Stahl walked off toward an idling Horch 901, where his driver was waiting. Moltke watched him go, then turned and made his way back to the half-track. He looked around for his men, but he didn't see them anywhere. *No matter*, he thought to himself. *They*

*were useless, anyway. But what now? Do I take a Gebirgsjäger
unit and look for the pilot around here, or do I go on ahead to the
border? And if the latter, where do I go?*

Before he could make up his mind, Moltke heard
someone call his name. He panicked, fearing the worst;
perhaps they'd realized that the pilot had already gotten
out of the country. He slowly turned around, but instead
of seeing Stahl or another superior officer, he saw the
scrawny man from Hegra, standing next to what looked
like a police motorcycle.

"Herr Oberleutnant?"

"What do you want?"

The man pulled the burnt scrap of the Allied
squadron patch from his pocket and showed it to Moltke,
then turned and nodded toward the mountains to the
southeast.

"I know which way they're going," he said.

CHAPTER 22

The black mountains rose in waves, churning and white-capped. They climbed ever higher to the east, each row more faded and illusory than the last. The darkening storm clouds sagged lower to meet them, making it difficult to tell the two apart. The world became a marbled, streaky palette, composed solely of greys.

Erling skied his way through the highlands, taking one long stride after another. He took advantage of the downhill stretches, crouching as he rushed headlong across untouched patches of snow. Going uphill, he shortened his stride and bent forward, leaning into the mountains. On a few of the steeper sections, he took off the skis and carried them over his shoulder, advancing slowly on foot.

He crossed another wide meadow, passing an old, snow-covered *seter*. A pair of gnarled pine saplings grew on its gently sloping roof, emerging from the sod and ice. In the summer months, the *seter*'s owner would likely return with his herd, and the animals would graze there until the days grew shorter again. For now, though, the area was a desolate and uninhabited wasteland.

Erling struggled his way up another hill, pushing the skis out as far as he could to lengthen his stride. He marched his way upward through the ankle-deep snow, fighting to keep his momentum and leaving a jagged herringbone pattern in his wake. When he finally reached the summit, a familiar vista lay before him. There was Fjelldalshøgda, shaped like a slumbering bear, and nearby was its tree-covered neighbor, Midtkveldslumpen. Finnhaugen and Tjønnmorya lurked beyond them, to the south, and in the distance, the high peak of Steinfjellet towered above everything else.

He scanned the horizon for Kari, or for any signs of where she might have gone, but there was nothing to be seen. There were no signs of man anywhere, for that matter; there were no buildings or roads, no tracts of cleared land or rising columns of smoke. The world before him was composed solely of mountains and ice. The only living things he could see were the trees; the place even seemed to be devoid of wildlife.

Erling continued on his way, coasting down another decline before climbing Tritjønnan. It wasn't difficult ascending it, but when he reached its peak, he saw that it fell off sharply on the other side. He looked back behind him, surveying the rugged landscape. He could backtrack and go around, heading south toward the marshy lowlands, or he could head north toward the less-rugged steppe. Either way would cost him a few hours, if not more, and as far as he was concerned, a few hours might be the difference between catching up to Kari and missing her altogether.

After mulling it over for a moment, Erling slowly went forward, descending the slope step by agonizing step. He walked sideways, relying on the makeshift poles for support. The rocky face of the hill was covered with ice, and a few times, he began to slip. He'd pause and steady himself before continuing, carefully raising and lowering each ski.

A few dozen steps into the journey, Erling began to breathe easier, settling into a routine. He found traction along cracks in the ice or in the rock itself, using all of his limbs and picking his way like a spider across a web. Meter by meter, step by step, the bottom of the valley came slowly into view. Glancing behind him, he watched the peak recede into the distance, then looked forward again, concentrating on his descent.

Halfway down the slope, Erling stepped onto a patch of black ice and started to slide. He turned around and tried to find his footing, but instead of regaining his purchase, the rocks gave out from underneath him. He began to slide backward down the hill, and as he struggled to turn around, he picked up more speed. He turned his skis inward, trying to stop, but it was no use— the ice was slick and the slope was steep, and he was already going so fast that he was skipping across the surface.

Surrendering to the idea of skiing his way down, Erling lowered into a crouch. He hadn't downhill skied in years, and his legs felt stiff and uncertain. He leaned and bent his way around rocks and ice in his path, trailing the makeshift poles behind him. As his speed accelerated, he found himself steering less and less and just struggling to remain on his feet.

He soon regained control, keeping his center of gravity as low as possible. He scraped his way down the face of the mountain, remembering to go with gravity and momentum rather than fight against it. For a moment, he almost forgot himself, lost in the speed and the rush of the descent. He felt like he was flying, a feeling he'd loved as a boy when he'd barrel recklessly down Strætasfjellet with his friends.

His short-lived moment of nostalgia ended when he spotted the fast-approaching trees and the icy lake beyond them. He suddenly felt all the air escape him, and he felt his heart begin to thud in his chest. He turned his skis inward again and tried to slow down, but he only picked up more speed as he skipped along the ice. Realizing he wouldn't be able to stop in time, he threw the bow and arrows toward a snow bank so they wouldn't break or injure him. Then he sat down and fell onto his back.

Erling skidded down the hill in a clashing of skis and ice. He struggled to keep his legs straight so his skis wouldn't cross, but it was no use. They tangled up, sending him tumbling toward the tree line. He came down hard on his side, cracking a rib and bruising his kidneys. He stopped trying to use the skis to break his slide and went with the fall, letting go of the poles and allowing his arms to trail behind him. His right ski popped off as he rolled toward the trees, and soon after that, his left ski came off as well.

Erling finally came to a stop just short of the lake, near a snow-covered mound of earth. Dazed and battered, he sucked for air. Once he got his bearings, he examined himself. The rocks and ice had cut his hands and hip, and there were long tears in his pants and coat.

He struggled to his feet. Then he limped back up the hill to gather his things, his bad knee feeling like someone had smashed it with a hammer. He was glad to see that the bow was intact, as were the arrows. The binding on his left ski was gone, however, and the ski itself was snapped in two.

Erling stepped into his remaining ski and pulled the binding tight. He then set off again, teetering upon the one remaining ski, his left foot raised and tucked like a crane's. He soon heard a buzzing sound in the distance; at first, it sounded like another plane, but he quickly realized it was the sound of an approaching ground vehicle. He struggled his way over to a stand of thick pines, hiding beneath their drooping boughs.

Then he watched as a Waffen-SS half-track approached in the distance, barreling toward the Swedish border.

The lakes turned silver in the waning daylight, and the ice that covered them made cracking noises as the temperature fell. Overhead, dull clouds hung low and thick, splitting against the distant mountaintops. They buried the emergent moon underneath a thick cataract of grey.

Kari and Lance continued their way eastward through the highlands. They'd ridden all day without stopping, and neither had said a word since they'd set out. Kari sat in front, loosely holding the reins; Lance sat behind her, his hands on her hips. The only sound aside from the shifting ice was the steady crunching of Torden's footfalls beneath them.

They rode over a series of low hills and into a shallow valley. On a few occasions, Kari had wanted to break the silence, but every time the urge came over her, she grew nervous and queasy, unable to think of anything that wouldn't sound naïve or immature. After cresting another ridge, she spotted Steinfjellet and Litlkluken, and just beyond them, she saw the peaks of Blåhammarfjället and

Snasahögarna, on the other side of the border. Though somewhat relieved, she also felt her heart sinking, knowing that their journey was coming to a close.

Kari thought back to the first time she'd been to Sweden, as a girl. She had vague memories of riding there with her parents, nestled next to her mother on the narrow seat of their horse-drawn cart. She couldn't remember much about the trip, but she could recall the soft feeling of her mother's worn cotton dress, and the fragrant smell of soap on her mother's skin. She could also remember the songs her mother sang on the way, *Å blei d'a dei (din blei)?*, *Det Er Min Egen Lille Hemmelighet,* and others by Lalla Carlsen. Then she thought about the last time she'd been there, the previous summer. While her father had been selling their wool, she'd met a boy named Mats, who was a child compared to Lance, but he'd had a certain charm. He'd wanted her to come to a fair with him, but her father had forbidden it, wanting to leave after he'd finished his business. She was so angry that she didn't speak to Erling the entire ride back, cursing God for taking her mother instead of him. The thought suddenly occurred to her that her father needed to bury himself with work in order to get past his grief. She began to finally understand him, and for a moment, she even started to feel sorry for him. Then she quickly pushed the thoughts from her mind, unwilling to let them alter her course.

They rode onward, crossing a frozen creek. Torden's hooves broke through the thin ice atop its surface, revealing the shallow water beneath. They soon entered a stretch of bare hardwoods. After the trees began to thin out, they clambered their way up another ridge, and when they reached the top, Kari spotted a few lights in the distance. Before long, Lance spotted them as well.

"Is that Sweden?" he asked.

She nodded. They continued on in silence, and a light snow began to fall, fine as sifted meal and nearly invisible in the fading light. They could hardly even feel it, melting as soon as it landed on their faces and hands.

They made their way up another low ridge and descended toward a flat valley. A handful of bare trees rose from the ground, thin as bones, and as they crossed the frozen wasteland, their shadows lengthened before them, becoming indistinct and fanning apart. They soon climbed again, up another low ridge hemmed with evergreen scrub. After reaching the crest, Kari heard a buzzing noise somewhere behind them, faint as a mosquito. She instinctively looked back toward the sky, but there was nothing there, other than a few darkening storm clouds.

"What is it?" asked Lance.

"I don't know," she said.

They scanned the horizon, looking for the origin of the sound. The buzzing noise grew louder and louder, and it sounded faster, too, and more like a car or truck engine than an aircraft. Torden grew nervous and tried to go back down the ridge, but Kari sawed at the reins and swung him around. Then she turned and looked behind them again and spotted an approaching half-track in the distance, barreling toward them. Lance's eyes widened when he saw it, too.

"Go," he said.

Kari yanked on the reins and dug her heels into Torden's ribs, and the horse struggled his way up and over the steep pitch of rock. He clambered over the broken ridge and down the other side, trotting downhill toward a treeless meadow. Halfway across the meadow, Kari glanced back over her shoulder. She saw the half-track hammering down the hill, shredding the distance between them.

Kari dug her heels into Torden's side again and yanked on the reins, and he broke into a gallop. There was no cover out in the meadow, but there was a steep ridge a hundred meters to the south. She wheeled the horse around and charged for the ridge, hazing Torden on as the half-track gained on them. After they reached the ridge, Torden fought his way up the rocks. Kari urged him onward, slapping him across the side, and Lance spun around and drew his pistol, but before he could find a shot, Torden stumbled on the ice and lost his footing. Kari fell backward against Lance, knocking the pistol loose and sending it clattering down the ridge.

The half-track pulled so close that they could see the rank insignia on the shoulder straps of Moltke's uniform and the *Totenkopf* on his hatband. Kari whacked Torden again and again, but the hill was too steep and the ground was too icy. Torden soon lost his footing, and Kari and Lance were thrown from the horse. She landed in a snowdrift, and Lance went down hard on his side.

They struggled to their feet and continued on as the half-track drew near, and when the half-track could go no further, Moltke skidded it to a halt and jumped out, chasing them on foot. Without breaking stride, Kari glanced back over her shoulder. She saw Moltke, brandishing a pistol. Sverre followed, struggling to keep up.

"*Stehen bleiben!*" shouted Moltke.

Kari and Lance ignored him, and he fired a shot over their heads.

"Stop!" he shouted. "*Stehen bleiben!*"

They continued to ignore him, running as fast as they could across the highlands. After cresting a hill, Kari spotted a tree line on the other side of a meadow, and she and Lance changed directions and bolted for the trees. Halfway across the meadow, Kari twisted her ankle in a rut and went down hard against her side, losing her wind. Lance stopped and looked back toward the approaching men, then looked toward Kari, on the ground.

"Sorry," he said.

Before she could reply, he turned and continued on. Kari struggled to scream, her panic turning to fury, but all she could manage was a weak groan. She watched as Lance ran off, part of her in shock, and another, larger part of her enraged. Before she could get back to her feet, though, Moltke and Sverre reached her, and Moltke grabbed her by the arm and shoved her toward Sverre.

"Stay here," he said.

Kari tried to pull free, but Sverre spun her around and hugged her tight, refusing to let go. She watched as Moltke closed the distance on Lance, firing another warning just above Lance's head. Lance ducked and slipped, and Moltke gained on him.

He caught up to Lance at the bottom of a ridge. Then he tackled him to the ground and smashed him in the head with his pistol.

CHAPTER 23

They trudged through the snow back in the direction of the half-track. Lance walked out front, blood leaking from his nostrils and split lip; Kari trailed nearby, staying as far away from Lance as their captors would allow. Both were bound at the wrists with coarse rope, and Moltke had tied it so tightly that their wrists bled.

Kari turned to face Sverre.

"You don't have to do this," she said, addressing him in Norwegian.

Moltke responded in German before Sverre could reply.

"Shut up," he said.

Kari continued, ignoring him.

"You should be helping us—"

Before she could finish, Moltke stepped forward and smashed her in the back of head with his pistol. She stumbled and took a knee, dazed.

"I said shut up," said Moltke.

Lance took a step toward Moltke, but when Moltke pointed the pistol at him, Lance froze, his bound hands leaping up to his face like the hands of a fevered supplicant.

"You want to be a hero?" said Moltke, in English.

"No," said Lance, cowering.

"Get her up."

Lance bent down to help Kari, but she swatted his hands away, standing on her own. Moltke shoved her.

"Move," he said.

They slogged onward. Lance continued to look over toward Kari, but she refused to meet his gaze. She scanned their surroundings for options, but there were none to be found. They were in the middle of a barren meadow; there was nowhere to run or hide, and nothing that could be used as a weapon, other than rocks buried in ice or the occasional stick.

After cresting a low hill, Kari spotted the half-track in the distance. She knew their time was running out; as soon as they reached the vehicle, their few options would all but disappear. She figured she was already living on borrowed time, anyway; the only one of any interest to the Nazis was Lance, and whether she was brought back alive, dead, or even at all seemed to be of little consequence.

She considered her options one last time. Making a run for it seemed like suicide; even if she'd somehow made it to the trees, she was bound and without a weapon, not to mention in the middle of nowhere. Going along with it and hoping for clemency only seemed like a slower journey to the same result, as they executed people or sent them to work camps for far lesser violations. The only solution as she saw it was to fight; if she'd somehow managed to overpower Moltke and take his weapon, she could surely take care of Sverre, who would likely cow to whoever was in control of the situation. If Lance helped her, great, but if not, as long as he stayed out of her way, she figured she had a chance. It was better than hoping or waiting for a miracle, which to her seemed like having no chance at all.

Her heart began to flutter and swell. She closed her eyes and took a deep breath, trying to still her nerves. She thought about praying, but what would she pray for, and to whom or to what would she pray? She didn't believe in anything, and she couldn't remember the prayers she'd learned in Sunday school as a girl, before her mother had died and her father had stopped bringing her to church.

She thought about her mother for a moment. *She believed in something, even in her final, dying days, but what did it get her?* Kari wondered. Maybe that wasn't the point in belief, she suddenly realized; maybe the point was that it gave one the strength to endure things rather than to change or escape them. She felt a sense of calmness wash over her, and felt her hammering heart begin to slow. *I'm with you now*, she could imagine her mother saying, in her calm and steady voice. *I always have been, and I always will be.*

Kari took one more deep breath and slowly let it out. Then, after steeling herself, she spun around and lunged toward Moltke, tackling him at the waist. They went tumbling to the ground, wrestling for control of the pistol. Sverre moved to help Moltke, but Lance shoved him to the snow.

Kari and Moltke struggled for the pistol as Lance blocked Sverre. Moltke dominated Kari, using his weight to overpower her. She caught him with his guard down and kneed him in the groin, and he rolled off her, sucking for air. Then she wrestled the gun free, but before she could use it, Moltke head-butted her in the face and flipped her onto her back. He grabbed the pistol and scrambled back to his feet, pointing it at Lance.

"Stay back!" shouted Moltke.

Lance moved away, cowering. Moltke turned back toward Kari and kicked her in the ribs. Lance watched helplessly as Moltke kicked her again and again. Then Moltke pointed the pistol at her, but before he could pull the trigger, Sverre grabbed him by the arm.

"Wait—"

Before Sverre could finish, Moltke pointed the pistol at him.

"I said stay back!" Moltke shouted.

Sverre backed away, and Moltke turned back toward Kari, who lay motionless in the snow. He pointed the pistol at her again and cocked its hammer, but before he could shoot, the head of an arrow burst through the center of his chest. Moltke slowly raised his free hand and touched the sharp point of the arrowhead, dumbfounded at the sight of the bright red blood. The others turned and looked in the direction the arrow had come from, spotting Erling atop a ridge, holding a bow and nocking another arrow. Kari shouted when she saw him.

"Dad!"

Lance looked toward Kari, confused, then back to Erling, watching as Erling loosed the arrow. It pierced Moltke near the base of his spine, and Moltke pitched forward to the snow, falling like a puppet whose strings had just been cut.

"Get the gun," shouted Erling.

Kari lunged for the pistol and reached it first, but before she could point it at Sverre, he tackled her, and they hit the ground in a heap. Kari looked to Lance.

"Don't just stand there," she said.

Lance lunged for Sverre, but before he could reach him, Sverre wrested the pistol from Kari and pointed it at Lance's head.

"That's far enough," he said.

Lance backed away as Sverre yanked Kari to her feet. Sverre then spun Kari around toward Erling, using her as a shield.

"Lower the bow," said Sverre.

"Don't do this," said Erling, nocking another arrow as he descended the ridge on his way toward them.

Sverre put the pistol to Kari's head.

"I said the lower the bow!" he shouted.

Erling continued to approach them.

"Stay back—!"

Before Sverre could finish, Kari kneed him in the crotch and pulled free, diving to the ground. Sverre lunged toward Kari, but Erling drew back on the bowstring and loosed the arrow before he could, hitting Sverre in the throat. Sverre spun and fired wildly at Erling, reaching for his gushing throat with his other hand. He quickly emptied the pistol, missing with every shot. Then he turned and scrambled off toward a nearby ridge, and Erling followed him, drawing another arrow.

Nearby, Moltke watched them from where he lay in the snow. He opened his mouth to speak, but no words came, and he gurgled up a mouthful of blood. He tried to get up, but his legs wouldn't move. He looked up again toward the others, but all he saw were a few hazy shapes. The edges of his vision grew blurry, like a clear fire was spreading across the earth. All the pain was draining away, but so was something else. His life force, if there was such a thing. He'd never given much thought to matters of the spirit, though, and it was too terrifying for him to consider them now.

Unwilling to think about it, he struggled to his back

and watched the clouds drift by, again recalling the *Wolkenatlas* from his days at the *Kriegsakademie*, when his life was still ahead of him. One of the clouds looked like a flexing arm, then swelled and straightened out into the shape of Italy. He'd always wanted to go to Rome, with Elise, and to look at the art in the Capitoline museum, and to get drunk on cheap Italian wine. Suddenly realizing that he'd never get the chance, he tried again to struggle to his feet, but once again, his legs refused. Then so did his lungs. He started to panic, unable to breathe. *I shouldn't be here*, he thought to himself. *I should be in Africa with Rommel, leading a column of Panzers against the Allies.*

A moment later, everything went black.

Erling trudged up the ridge, following the blood trail in the snow. He held the arrow nocked and ready, but he kept the bowstring slack, hoping he wouldn't have to use it. In a few a places, it looked like Sverre had regained his strength and was making a run for it, as his tracks grew further and further apart. In others, though, it looked like he'd fallen or was running out of steam; his footprints became frantic, the snow packed down and stained with blood.

The trail tightened, and the gaps between the spatter grew shorter and shorter the further he went. Before long, he was following a near continuous line, a messy crimson ellipsis in the snow. After cresting the hill, Erling spotted

Sverre in the distance, sitting against a bare and gnarled tree. Sverre had become as pale as the snow around him, and he clutched the side of his neck, trying in vain to suppress the wound.

Erling lowered the bow and slowly approached his old friend. Sverre looked up at Erling and smiled as he came near, as if they were meeting under vastly different circumstances. For some reason, Erling thought back to the time they'd run off as thirteen year-olds to join the army during the early days of World War I, after a German U-boat had sunk the *Ulriken* and killed a local who'd been part of her crew. Sverre had been the only other one who hadn't turned around and gone back home along the way, and they'd made it all the way to Oslo before they'd finally gotten caught.

After a moment, Sverre opened his mouth to speak. Instead of any words coming out, he gurgled up a bright red bubble of blood. He closed his mouth, then opened it again and hesitated for a long moment, as if considering what to say. After another moment, he let out a quick, aching sigh, and then he went still, his vacant eyes fixed on the horizon.

Kari came up over the ridge behind Erling and saw Sverre. A moment later, Lance followed.

"Is he dead?" asked Kari.

Erling nodded.

"I'm sorry—"

He interrupted her.

"We should hide the bodies," he said.

Lance followed Erling back down the hill to get Moltke's body. Erling took the pistol from Moltke and stuffed it into his waistband, then reached under Moltke's armpits while Lance grabbed Moltke by the ankles. They lifted the body and carried it up the ridge, bringing it to a shelf of land just above the trail. Then they carried Sverre's body there as well.

Erling found a large, flat rock and began to dig into the ground. The earth was frozen solid and difficult to dig into, and they took turns until they'd dug a pit deep enough to bury the bodies. Erling went through Moltke's pockets and took out everything that could identify him. Then he went through Sverre's pockets. He found two coins, a dried rusk of brown bread, and a child's jackknife. In Sverre's coat, he found a creased and faded photograph of a girl that looked like it had been taken when they were young. Erling recognized the girl, but he couldn't remember her name. *Was it Solveig, or Sofie?* he wondered. He wasn't sure, but he knew she'd married a schoolteacher from Lånke and moved out west decades before. He'd never known that Sverre had been fond of her, though the picture had clearly been taken during the time that he and Sverre had been close. It made him wonder about all the other things he hadn't known about Sverre, and about everyone else, too, for that matter, and what they didn't know about him. People seemed to be full of hidden fires, invisible to one another and often even invisible to oneself.

Erling slipped the photograph into his pocket along with the rest of Sverre's things. Then he rolled the bodies into the shallow grave, one after the other.

CHAPTER 24

The night cold thickened the highlands, stiffening the grass and putting hoarfrost on the trees. Its winds made an icy music as they swept down from the mountaintop, rattling branches and scraping across the hardening ground.

They drove the half-track west, back in the direction it had come. They took a meandering route, crossing and recrossing the earlier tracks in case the Germans came looking for Moltke. Luckily for them, it began to snow again, and the winds soon raged. Before long, it became difficult to tell which tracks were the most recent, and soon after that, which were even tracks at all.

Erling stopped when they approached Tjønnmorya, where they found Torden milling about in an open meadow, favoring his right side. Kari and Lance got out of the half-track and approached him while Erling continued on, driving the half-track up a hill overlooking the Mikkelstjønnan lakes. At the top of the hill, Erling turned around the half-track and pointed it toward one of the lakes. Then he got out of the half-track and looked for a heavy stone. Once he found one, he took the can of gas, a rifle, and some ammunition from the back of the half-track. Then he wedged the stone against the half-track's gas pedal and shifted it into gear.

The half-track lurched over the crest of the hill and began hurtling toward the lake, picking up speed as it barreled down the hill. It rumbled out onto the ice and broke through the surface, churning forward through the freezing water. It began to lose speed as the water rose up over its wheels, and then its doors, and then flooded into its seating area. Then it disappeared beneath the surface, and a glut of bubbles rose up, signaling the termination of its engine.

Erling slung the rifle over his shoulder. Then he walked down the hill and out into the meadow, where he joined the others. Torden pulled free from Kari and hobbled over toward Erling, ecstatic to see him. Erling put down the gas can and rubbed Torden's neck, and the horse nuzzled and licked him, hungry for his touch.

Erling pulled out the rusk of bread he found in Sverre's pocket and gave it to Torden, who gummed it down. After he massaged Torden's ears and neck for a moment, Erling bent down and looked over Torden's hooves. The left front hoof was bleeding, and it looked like he'd walked across a field of jagged rocks. The left rear hoof was even worse, laced with deep slices and nearly cracked in half. Erling cleaned them out as best as he could and patched them with sap. Then he tore the rest of his undershirt in half and fashioned a pair of makeshift bandages for Torden's hooves.

Once he finished taking care of the horse, Erling and the others gathered Moltke's and Sverre's things into a pile and dumped gasoline onto it. Then they set it aflame. After watching the fire dwindle down to ashes, they kicked snow over it until they'd buried it. Then they turned and began walking in the direction of Sweden.

Erling held Torden's reins, guiding him over the rough terrain. They walked without speaking, each lost in their own separate world. Erling wanted to tell Kari he was glad she was all right, and that he wasn't angry, but he didn't know how; he kept thinking of Martha, and how much Kari reminded him of her, of her stubbornness and the way she fought for things she believed in. Kari, on the other hand, wanted to apologize to Erling for the trouble she'd caused, and to tell him that he'd been right, but her pride wouldn't allow it. Lance burned with his own regrets, and there were so many things he'd wanted to say to Kari, but he didn't know where or how to begin. Though they were only an arm's length away from one another, it felt like they were miles apart, and the longer they went without speaking, the more impenetrable the silence became.

Eventually, the snowfall began to cease, and not long afterward, the storm clouds broke, dissipating in the wind. The waning moon appeared, a smear of jaundiced light in an otherwise colorless sky. The stars soon returned as well. They could see Hrungnir's huge, odd-shaped heart, and Thjálfi fighting Mökkurkálfi until the end of time, and Freyr's great boar Gullinbursti, with his long, twisting mane.

They ascended a low ridge and wandered across a frozen bog. The ice was thick with branches and logs, and they slipped and stumbled their way through the mire. After crossing the swamp, they spotted a large, kidney-shaped lake in the distance; the silver reflection of the moon shone upon its surface, dull as an old coin. Erling stopped and looked at the lake, and then at the mountains behind them. After a moment, Kari and Lance stopped as well, turning and looking toward Erling.

"What is it?" asked Kari.

Erling nodded toward the mountains just beyond the lake.

"That's Sweden," he said.

"Hot damn," said Lance.

Erling leaned the rifle against a tree. Then he reached under his sweater and pulled out a gold ring suspended on a chain. He took off the ring and chain and offered them to Kari.

"What's this?" she asked.

"You're going to need it," he said, taking off his own battered wedding ring and offering it to her as well.

"Hold on—"

He interrupted her.

"Norway's not safe for you anymore," he said. "You've been wanting to leave, anyway. Now you have an excuse."

"But it's not safe for you, either," she said.

"Nobody saw me with him," said Erling, nodding toward Lance. "Besides, someone's got to look after the herd."

"Dad—"

He interrupted her again.

"It's done," he said, putting the rings into her palm and closing her fingers over them. "Now get going before I change my mind."

He lifted her up and put her onto Torden's back, then turned to Lance, handing him the rifle.

"Get her to an Allied base, and tell them what she did for you," he said.

"Yes, sir," said Lance, climbing up onto the horse behind her.

Erling turned back to Kari, speaking to her in Norwegian.

"Look up your uncle in New Jersey," he said. "He'll take you in."

"Wait," she began, choking up with tears.

Before she could finish, Erling slapped Torden on the rear end, and the horse trotted off to the east. He watched her go, then turned and walked off into the shadows, heading west back in the direction of the Stjørdalen Valley.

CHAPTER 25

Dawn steeped into the sky, and the mountains emerged from the blue-black night. A halting breeze came to life, kicking up the snow and rousing the birds from their nests. A few of them took flight, heading west and disappearing into the cloudbanks.

Kari and Lance continued their way toward the border. She sat out in front, holding the reins. Lance sat behind her, giving her as much space as he could without falling off the horse. Every time he brushed up against her, she stiffened as if he were probing her with a hot poker. He opened his mouth to speak a few times, but he couldn't think of anything to say, so he ended up not saying a word.

They rode onward, soon cresting a low ridge and heading down into a valley. Torden stumbled on a patch of rocky ice and slid a few paces before regaining his footing. Lance nearly fell off the horse and grabbed onto Kari's side for support. Once he steadied himself, she shrugged him off, repelled by his touch.

After a while, Lance finally spoke.

"Listen," he said, "about what happened—"

She interrupted him before he could finish.

"I don't want to talk about it," she said.

"I wouldn't have left you—"

She interrupted him again.

"I said I don't want to talk about it," she said.

He opened his mouth to speak again but decided against it, and they continued on in silence. Overhead, the sky became suffused with more and more light until it became a pale shade of violet. The wind faded away, and wet wads of snow began to fall from the boughs of the evergreens. A bird cried in the distance, its lonely song piercing the emptiness.

They made their way across the uneven landscape, fording frozen creeks and trudging up shelves of icy rock. After a while, Lance began to sing.

> *"You're the cream in my coffee,*
> *You're the salt in my stew,*
> *You'll always be my necessity,*
> *I'd be lost without you…"*

This time, Kari didn't laugh. She didn't smile, or soften, or have any reaction at all. Lance no longer seemed like Clark Gable to her, or Cary Grant, or even the stars of the B-movies they used to put on the lower halves of the double features at the Rosendal. He was just like Håkon and Jan Petter and the others, or even worse in that he'd pretended to be something more.

They rode onward. The sun continued to rise and swell, fighting its way through the wall of clouds. Ribbons of low fog broke up and dissipated in the easterly wind, and mixed flocks of wheatear and starlings pecked at the softening snow.

They soon climbed another rise and picked their way across a rutted meadow. The frozen bushes and shrubs crunched loudly beneath Torden's hooves. They entered a forest of old birch and spruce trees, and after the trees thinned out, they rode toward the crest of another hill. At its peak, Kari saw a cluster of houses in a valley to the northeast. Thin columns of smoke rose from a few chimneys and flattened out in the breeze.

They continued on, down the hill and through another forest. At the forest's edge, they dismounted and tied Torden to a tree. Then they went forward and looked out toward the village. They watched it for almost an hour, and they didn't see a single soldier or any other sign of the Germans.

They eventually spotted a middle-aged man making his way toward an old wood-frame church. They waited a few more minutes, then left their weapons by Torden and ventured out toward the church. Halfway there, they saw another man coming up the road from the other side of the village, riding a horse-drawn cart. They slowed, expecting the worst, but the man continued past on his cart, paying them no mind.

As soon as the man was gone, Kari and Lance approached the church and went inside. It was quiet and dark, and there didn't appear to be anyone there. They wandered past the wooden pews lining the nave and approached the modest altar. Before they reached it, a woman emerged from the sacristy, carrying a stack of worn hymnals. She nearly dropped them, startled by their presence.

"May I help you?" she said, speaking in Swedish, which was similar enough to Norwegian for Kari to understand.

"This man is an American pilot," said Kari, in English.

"Oh my," said the woman, putting down the stack of hymnals. "Wait here. I'll get the reverend."

Lance looked to Kari as the woman hurried off, concerned.

"Don't worry," she said.

They waited, and after a moment, the woman returned from the back of the church followed by the middle-aged man they'd seen before. His thick coat was off, revealing a shirt with a clerical collar, and he addressed them in a thick and halting English.

"Welcome," he said, extending his hand. "I'm Pastor Lundqvist."

"Major Lance Mahurin of the 56th," said Lance,

shaking the pastor's hand.

"We can help you," said the pastor.

He led Lance toward a hallway, and the woman followed them. Kari hesitated, remaining behind. She looked toward the altar, which was dressed for a service, then looked back to the hallway, where Lance and the others disappeared into a room. She thought about America, and her uncle Agnar, and everything she'd seen in the movies. Then she thought about her father and their farm back in the Stjørdalen Valley.

After a long moment, she turned and headed toward the door.

CHAPTER 26

Kari made her way back across the village, walking as quickly as possible. A part of her wanted to run, but she kept her speed in check, not wanting to draw any attention. Rounding a corner, she approached a man shoveling snow outside his store. The man looked up and nodded to her as she passed by, and she nodded back as she continued on her way.

She soon left the village and approached the forest. Torden nickered when he saw her, tugging at his reins and shifting excitedly from side to side. She went over to him and stroked him under his jaw, talking into his ear in a low and steady voice. He nuzzled into her, grateful for her touch.

Kari picked up the rifle. Then she hesitated, uncertain. It seemed like more trouble than it was worth; there'd be no way to explain to the Germans why she had it, if they'd found her with it, and she couldn't think of many situations where having it might actually make a difference.

After a long moment, Kari put down the rifle. Then she untied Torden from the tree. She mounted him and took the reins, then gently kicked his flanks.

Torden turned and trotted off toward the mountains to the west, as if he knew exactly where he was going.

A biting, down country wind swept the last grey storm clouds from the sky. Dusk came cold and blue, settling in over the mountains. It was clear enough to see the rough texture of the emerging moon, and the faint outlines of the goshawks and harriers that crossed over it. They swooped in and out of the light, scouring the valley below for prey.

Kari rode her way westward through the highlands, taking the same route they'd taken on their way east. Their earlier tracks were gone, long since erased and smoothed over by the chafing wind. There was no sign of civilization or man out there at all, just mountains and trees and ice. It was as quiet as the bottom of the ocean; the only sound that broke the vast silence was the steady clop of Torden's hooves in the frozen snow.

They rode up a low ridge and down toward a wooded gap. Then they entered the forest. Before long, Kari heard the sound of footsteps somewhere in the shadows before them. She pulled up on the reins, jerking

Torden to a halt. A moment later, a wolf emerged from the trees just ahead of them, its yellow-gold eyes glinting in the darkness.

They stayed where they were and watched each other, both parties cautious and curious at the same time. The wolf was so close that Kari could smell its rancid breath and its wet, gamy hair. After a moment, in a show of intimidation, the wolf bared its teeth and began to growl. Kari held her ground, massaging Torden's neck and whispering calmly into his ear, keeping eye contact with the wolf the entire time.

After another moment, the wolf stopped growling. Then it turned and trotted off, and Kari and Torden continued on their way.

Dawn came slowly, like someone was dripping milk into a bucket of ink. When the sun finally showed itself, there were no clouds to dampen it, and it turned the sky a pearly shade of blue. The snow began to soften, dropping in clumps from the boughs of the trees. Goldcrest and chaffinch passed through the valley on their way back north, singing their rusty song.

Kari rode westward through the hills, bleary-eyed and exhausted but somehow still awake. She'd ridden through the night, only stopping to water Torden at a creek and to refashion his bandages after they'd come apart. After they crested a low ridge and she saw the

Stjørdalen Valley in the distance, she perked up, reinvigorated. She even felt tears forming at the corner of her eyes, never so happy to see her home.

She made her way to the paved country road that ran from Hegra to Trondheim. Then she took it all the way until she got to the dirt trail that led to their farm. Along the journey, she played out the scene of her arrival over and over again in her head. In it, she'd watch her father emerge from the barn, where he'd be tending to the animals. Seeing her coming, he'd drop what he was doing and run to her. When he'd reach her, he'd scoop her up in his thick arms and lift her into the air, grinning from ear to ear. He'd carry her inside, and everyone from the valley would come join them, celebrating her return with a feast.

She rode onward, trying to contain her growing excitement. Tears began to form at the corners of her eyes again, but she blinked them away, not wanting to appear weak or sentimental. She soon began to smell smoke, and at first, she thought her father had a fire going. The further she went, though, the more acrid the smell became, soon reminding her of the scent of burning hair.

Kari kicked her heels into Torden's side, and he picked up his pace, galloping up the narrow cart path. The air grew hazy and grey, and the burning smell grew more pungent and sharp. Kari smacked Torden's side and dug her heels into his ribs, and he thundered his way through the forest. Approaching their farm, she felt like she'd been kicked in the gut when she saw it razed before her, reduced to rubble and ash.

She jumped off the horse and ran toward what had been their house. One of its walls had fallen over into the yard, shriveled and black; another was completely gone, and the roof had collapsed, leaving little standing other than the chimney and part of the back wall. Kari stepped over the threshold of the front door and walked through the rubble, looking for signs of her father. She found part of his bed frame, a curled up leather boot, and a burned jacket of his, but there was no sign of Erling anywhere.

After searching the house, she stumbled her way through the snow and over to their collapsed barn. Then she picked her way through its charred ruins. She found rake heads and hammer claws, the wooden handles of which had burned away. She found broken bottles and window glass, scorched black as coal. She found acrid lumps of burnt hair and gristle, too many to count. There was no sign of her father there, either, though she wasn't sure whether she should be relieved or worried even more. For all she knew, the Germans could've shipped him off to Falstad, or worse; he could be lying in a ditch somewhere, or hanging from a noose.

Kari hurried her way back to Torden, who nickered and stamped in the snow, clearly uncomfortable. She took the reins and swung up onto his back, then dug her heels into his side, riding her way back up the narrow cart path. She soon approached the Jacobsen's property; their farmhouse and barn had also been razed, and the tractor had been reduced to a blackened skeleton. She rode past the Prestrud farm after that, finding that it had also been burned to the ground.

She made her way back to the country road and set out for her Uncle Reidar's farm. She inwardly cursed herself along the way, blaming herself for what had happened. Her head swirled with dark thoughts, and she started to feel like she couldn't breathe. She pushed the thoughts from her mind, kicking her heels into Torden's ribs and riding him onward as fast as she could.

Kari soon turned onto the dirt road leading to her uncle's farm. She drove Torden on until she saw her uncle's barn appear in the distance, and then the mustard-colored farmhouse just beyond it. Seeing her cousins Erik and Ivar in the yard, she yanked on the reins and pulled Torden to a halt, jumping down off the horse before he'd even come to a stop. Then she ran toward them through the shin-deep snow, stumbling a few times and eventually falling before struggling back to her feet and continuing on.

She opened her mouth to speak as she approached Erik and Ivar, but before she could say anything, she heard a voice call her name nearby.

"Kari?"

She turned to see her father walking toward her from the barn.

"Dad?"

She ran to him and jumped into his arms, fighting

back the tears.

Erling held her tightly to his chest, fighting back tears of his own.

ACKNOWLEDGEMENTS

I'm indebted to Hans Christian Adamson's *Blood on the Snow*, Sigurd Evensmo's *A Boat For England*, William F. Fuller and Jack Haines' *Reckless Courage: The True Story of a Norwegian Boy Under Nazi Rule*, Odd Nansen's *Day After Day*, and Gunnar Sønsteby's *Report from #24*. I'm also indebted to the stories of my grandfather, Roy Zachary (1919-2005), who served in the Army Air Corps during WWII; my other grandfather, Norman Kjeldsen (1921-1992), and his brothers, Curtis Kjeldsen (1918-2005), and Harold Kjeldsen (1926-1944), who all served in the U.S. Armed Forces during WWII; and their cousins, Hans Christian Kjeldsen and Tore Kjeldsen, who lived in Norway during the German Occupation.

ABOUT THE AUTHOR

Kirk Kjeldsen received an MFA from the University of Southern California and is currently an assistant professor in the cinema program at Virginia Commonwealth University's School of the Arts. His first novel, *Tomorrow City*, was named one of the ten best books of 2013 by *The New Jersey Star-Ledger*. He also wrote and produced the feature film *Gavagai*, which was directed by Rob Tregenza. He lives in Essen, Germany with his wife and two children.